BECOMING MALKA

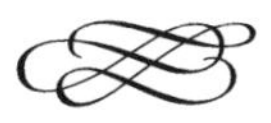

MIRTA INES TRUPP

Cover photo: Depositphotos.com

Although this author writes from a Jewish perspective, not every belief and doctrine expressed in this book may agree with the beliefs and doctrines of any of the three major Jewish branches.

Nevada, USA

CONTENTS

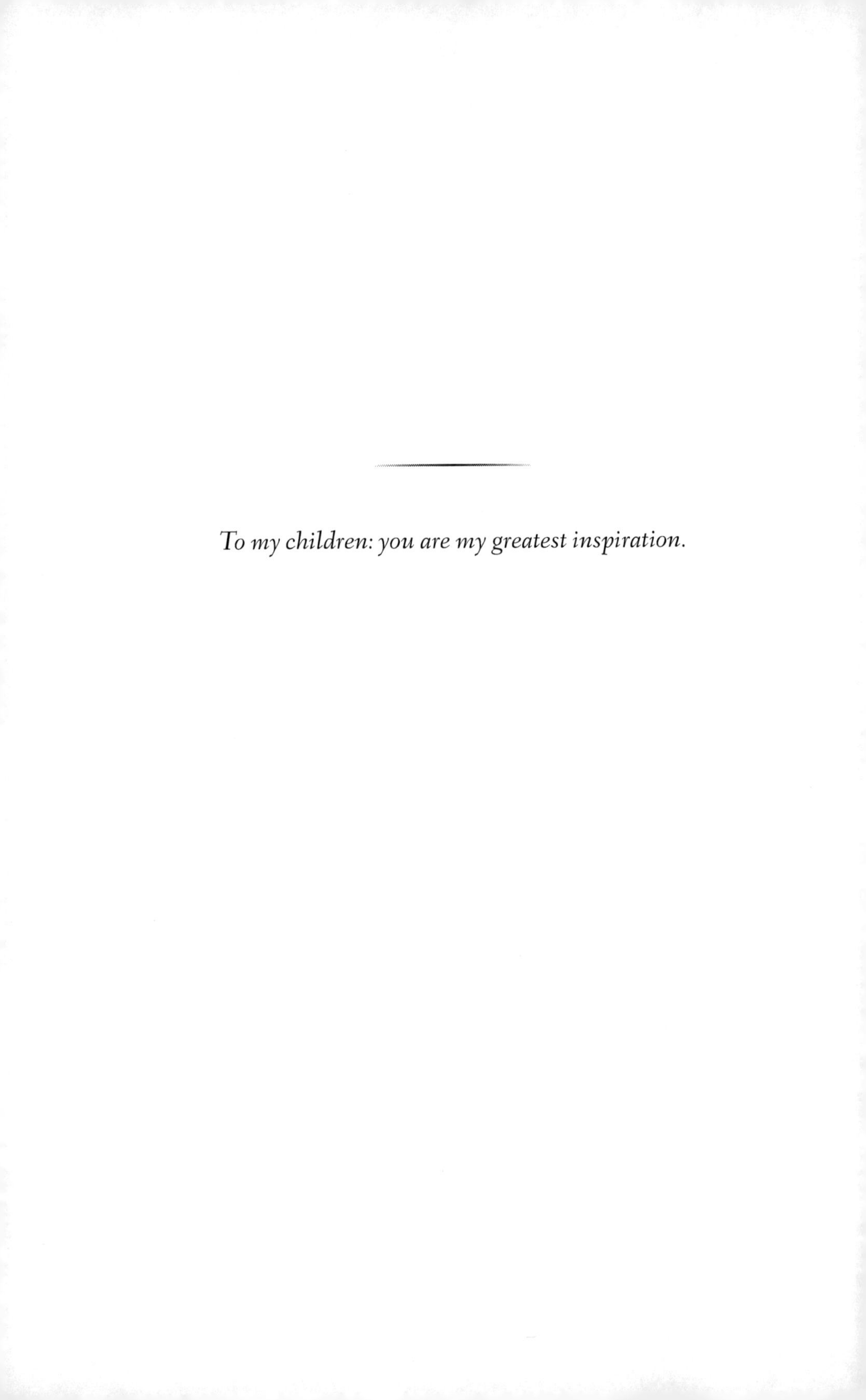

To my children: you are my greatest inspiration.

Your heart knows things that your mind can not explain.
~Author Unknown

FOREWORD

It was in early 2016 when an email appeared in my box from an author asking if I would read her story about self-discovery. Little did I know that story would introduce me to not only history, but also an amazing literary talent. As a writer, I know firsthand the hindrances that arise from being lavished with praise when seeking guidance. However, upon finishing my read of Becoming Malka, I had to know the author's plans going forward because the novel was very well written.

From the correspondence that followed, it was revealed that the author, whom I now know as Mirta, had a familial connection with the book's subject matter and retained plans to self-publish. When she asked me to consider writing a foreword, it sat me in my chair. Never have I been asked to write an introduction. My queries from authors have been solicited for reviews and once for a book's back cover. Therefore, I find it difficult to express how humbled I am to have the honor. To not detract, let me borrow your time to praise the pages you are about to enjoy.

A common trait that all good writers share is their ability to pull the reader in with a passion to turn the page. This is so important that some writing instructors claim the first sentence to a story legislates the power of the entire work. How's that for pressure?

As a beta reader, a person who reads manuscripts and offers advice, I read a lot of stories, and no two authors write the same. All have their own idiosyncrasies and merit. Still yet, there are some stories that stand out above others and deserve praise; Becoming Malka is one of them.

I could not put this manuscript down. I breezed through it in what seemed like hours. While some stories have left me guessing, Becoming Malka left me imagining. Through skillful use of prose and well-researched history pertaining to Jews living in Russia, Ukraine, and Argentina, the book is more than simply fiction. It is an educative resource that will enlighten the minds of all who read it.

Being one who does not enjoy spoiling a plot, I am going to end now and let you get to what I am convinced will not be a chore of a read. We put up with a lot on this amazing planet to remain content. Thankfully, there are those who write well to help us manage.

Brooks Kohler- M.A. in History

Author and Founder of Laptiast.com

Member of Phi Alpha Theta in the Field of History

CHAPTER ONE

7th of April

"Put seats in upright position. Captain announces descent." As all communication had been during the relatively brief flight, the flight attendant's instructions were short and to the point. They also lacked auxiliary verbs. "Soon to arrive in Odessa International Airport. Attendants come for port of entry forms."

Never one to have to be told twice, Molly adjusted her seat and had the requested forms readily available. She was more than ready to land; and surprisingly, it was not because she was excited to begin her research. The national airline proved to be just as one would have imagined. The flight was cheap. The food was just about average. And the service, well...it didn't come with a smile.

A student of all things Russian, Molly was certainly not caught off guard as other foreign passengers. They were not quite sure what to make of the so-called rude behavior and lackluster accommodations. She had learned through observation and experience that a "please" or a "thank you" would not earn a paying passenger access to the restroom before the flight attendants exercised their rights to use the facilities. Neither would a beguiling smile warrant the luxury of getting ice for their cola or an extra pillow to compensate for the thin, worn-out article of batting that had been provided.

Thankfully the five-hour flight from Moscow was relatively short, as the cramped seating arrangements did little to enhance the experience. The lack of leg room was in good company with the duct taped seats, as well as the outdated—yet provocative—uniforms that Oksana, Svetlana, and Tatiana modeled sauntering up and down the aisle. To be sure, the flight attendants were stunning; nonetheless, smiles were awarded as if they were a rationed item and communication in English was almost nonexistent.

After a whirlwind week of conferences and student activities in Moscow, Molly was excited for the second leg of her journey. Although she had enjoyed spending time with her colleagues and knew that the experience would prove beneficial for her master's thesis, she was looking forward to her own personal research in her ancestral home. Truth be told, she was looking forward to losing herself in a world of genealogy and history. Those treasured pastimes allowed her to escape the need to face the here and now.

At twenty-four years of age, Molly was the consummate student. There was always another class—another assignment. The level of discipline and organization required for advance studies fulfilled her need for structure and stability. She thrived in this environment. Projects were completed on time, lectures were given on point, and appointments were scheduled six months in advance in order to avoid the last-minute rush. Everything was neat and tidy, uncomplicated and predictable. Everything that is except for her boyfriend, Michael.

"Don't go to Russia," were his last words before she left. "Stay with me and let's elope to Las Vegas."

Michael Feldman wanted to get married. The same Michael Feldman who couldn't figure out what he was going to do with his life. No money put away. No long term plan. He was the dreamer, the do-gooder.

Michael was ready to pack a duffle bag and sign up to teach underprivileged kids in foreign countries, but she was the practical one who wanted a five-year plan. When she had asked where they would live or how would they support themselves, he shrugged his shoulders and said, "We'll figure it out as we go."

She was definitely not on board with that. She was not rushing into marriage or leaving the country without a timetable or mapped-out strategy. Life was hard. Life was daunting. They weren't prepared, financially or mentally—at least, she wasn't. To be precise: she wasn't ready to be a Malka.

Molly grew up in a loving household with a brilliant, but absent-minded professor as a father and a hippy dippy, all-you-need-is-love, artist for a mother. Her parents were bound together by faith and culture both having immigrated to the United States in the early sixties from a struggling Argentina.

Judith and David Abramovitz shared a love of music, food, and family, but they were as different as Charles Dickens was to Beatrix Potter. Where her father was a lover of all things history and quiet corners that called out for a good book and a cup of tea, her mother was a free spirit. She was a lover of New Age philosophies, of dancing in the rain and of breaking into song at the drop of a hat.

Delighted to find his daughter curious and receptive to family stories, David Abramovitz and young Molly would spend long cozy afternoons cuddled together in the library. She was weaned on the family's ancient history. These were stories about great-great-grandparents trekking across Mother Russia; and as Molly grew older and more inquisitive, he explained about the harsh realities of their lives.

He taught her about *pogroms*, anti-Semitism, and the era's volatile political situation. Molly had been fascinated to learn how her relatives boarded ships and sailed across the ocean to reach the shores of Argentina. David's great grandmother had made the journey. A widow, she left behind her husband's grave and followed her family as they made their way to "the New Jerusalem."

The stories of courage and determination both amazed and frightened Molly. In her eyes, the women of her father's stories were incredibly brave. They were made of sturdy stuff. They knew what was expected of them and they muddled through what could only be called extreme conditions. In her mind, the sheer thought of going off into the unknown, ill-prepared—with no money, no means of support, no language—was agony. But the matriarch didn't actually *follow* her family, as David related the story. She blazed the trail. She was their beacon of light and strength. She was the queen. She was Malka.

Molly's musings were interrupted as she adjusted her position for the hundredth time while avoiding a strip of duct tape protruding from the back of her seat. Once settled, she again contemplated the age-old question: how did her ancestors do it? *I am cut from a different cloth.*

She was the no-nonsense, no surprises, it's Monday-it-must-be-meatloaf, sort of girl. When she had completed her registration for the Moscow conference, she immediately set out to organize the side trip to Odessa. It wouldn't have been practical to traipse across the continents to Russia without making a pit stop in the neighboring country of Ukraine. She had funds allocated for such a trip, and had cleared her calendar to ensure she had sufficient time for both the conference and her genealogical research. *Give me a plan and I'm good to go.* Squaring her shoulders, she jutted her chin forward as much as a confirmation to her own statement as well as to brace herself for landing on terra firma.

The next few days were going to be a treat—a genealogist's dream come true—uninterrupted time for research and exploration. Molly promised herself that she'd think about Michael's proposal at some point. It had been an unexpected, yet sincere, offer. He deserved a response; but right now, she had to prepare for the gulag-style Customs at Odessa International. That was going to take some concentration and determination—and no smiles.

The airport had been built in the early sixties when Ukrainians were limited with regard to foreign travel. Molly hadn't expected much; therefore, she wasn't overly disappointed with either the architecture or interior design. But when she finally cleared the nightmare that was passport control and baggage claim, she cursed herself for listening to her Muscovite friends. They had convinced her not to prearrange for a private chauffer. Unexpectedly finding herself in a sea of seedy options,

Molly hailed a taxi and quickly jumped in an ancient Lada without take a moment to determine the condition of the vehicle.

Overwhelmed by the stench of *eau de Marlboro,* Molly unsuccessfully tried to roll down the passenger window before realizing the handle was broken. The remaining window had been busted out A sheet of black plastic wrap was duct taped around the opening. Although her language skills were near perfect, Molly was barely able to squeak out the name and address of the hotel as she gasped for a breath of fresh air.

The taxi driver peered through his rearview mirror, looked her up and down, and finally said, "Amerikansky?"

"Da," she croaked and tried not to panic. She should have stuck to her guns and made arrangements with a reputable transportation service. For some odd reason, her mother's words came to mind: *Relax, Molly love. Go with the flow.*

Relax? She wasn't even sure that the cabby was legitimate. She had seen to all the other arrangements. How did she let this one item slide?

When she couldn't reserve a room at the famed Hotel Bristol, the issue was easily resolved by a Russian colleague who recommended another option. It wasn't quite as fashionable, but it had decent accommodations and was centrally located. The same helpful colleague laughed when Molly turned down her invitation to the family's *dacha* outside of Moscow.

A group of the girls were planning to let loose on an extended weekend in the country, but Molly explained that she was not on vacation. She was on a working excursion through her ancestral home. She tried to not be hurt by the woman's laughter. It was not mean spirited; and to tell the truth, it came as no surprise that her interests were deemed rather unique.

While frittering away some free time at the conference, the girls scrolled through a social media site. Just for the fun of it, they took an online personality quiz. One of the questions asked: If you could share a meal with a historical figure or a fictional character, who would you choose? The options were Abraham Lincoln, Albert Einstein, Marilyn Monroe, or Captain James T. Kirk. The fifth selection was a blank field, which allowed the participant to enter a person of their choice. Much to the amusement of the others, Molly typed: My great-great-grandfather. Therefore, it should not have come as a surprise to her colleagues that while they were off gallivanting in the Khimki forest, Molly's next task was to contact Galina Alexsandrovich, a tour guide that came highly recommended by the Jewish Genealogical Society of Odessa.

Molly had corresponded with the organization via email and explained her unique request. Through a series of events, she had been able to track down the exact address of her family's last known residence—an estate now under the auspices of the historical society. Although she and her father chalked up the find to dedicated genealogists who happened to be in the right place at the right time, her mother, Judith, categorically declared that the discovery was a gift from Molly's spirit guides. In any event, whether by academia or spiritual intervention, Molly was determined that the family home would be her first stop. And to see that to fruition, she was instructed to contact Galina Alexsandrovich.

The Society complained that they were not funded sufficiently to maintain these historic properties, but Molly soon found that they managed to rake in a pretty penny. They were more than happy to charge an exorbitant entrance fee per visitor, and in addition, they required a house guide—a State-certified house guide, no less.

Galina Alexsandrovich owned an agency that provided Jewish heritage tours to foreigners. A local, she was quite knowledgeable and ran a lucrative business bringing in clientele from all over the world —a small, yet significant detail that proved to be beneficial. The Society enjoyed the trickle-down boost from her agency; and therefore, they didn't pursue the little matter of her certification. Galina was approved and assigned a key to the Abramovitz home.

As the taxi driver raced down Primorsky Boulevard, Molly shifted from one side to another, not wanting to miss any of the architectural attractions. Naturally, she had made a list of must-see places to visit: the Philharmonic Theater, the Opera House and the City Garden on Pushkinska Street. Aside from the family's home, her main point of interest was the Jewish quarter where she'd find the Jewish Museum of Odessa and the Great Choral Synagogue.

There were many places of worship in the city; but the Great Choral Synagogue, due to its history and architecture, was unquestionably the one to beat. The original structure from 1790 had been rebuilt after a fire destroyed the *beit tefillah* in 1840. During the Soviet period, the synagogue was seized and used as a sports hall for the general public. Eventually the Jewish community was able to reclaim and renovate the building, which was now being used as a religious and educational center. Molly was determined to spend some quality time in its famed library and research area.

The taxi driver's sharp turn brought her attention back to her current location. He made another turn and a rather brusque stop, before finally delivering Molly to her hotel. Having learned her lesson in Moscow, she gingerly placed the fare on the vehicle's dashboard and backed away—no smile. With bushy eyebrows lifting up high into his hairline, the driver couldn't mask his surprise. He was pleased the American knew that money could transmit negative energy. He ceremoniously tipped his hat and wished her a good day. Only when Molly stepped up onto the curb, and he was assured that the link was broken, did he gather the bills and place them in a worn leather satchel.

Taking a moment to admire the symmetrical stone façade, Molly marveled at the design of the relatively unknown building. She recognized the Renaissance Revival features shared by many of the city's legendary institutions. The cube-shape was reminiscent of the Great Choral Synagogue. The roof was topped with balustrade and the windows were trimmed in carved stone—each floor showcasing a different design. She had been disappointed when the Bristol turned her away; but as she entered the building and made her way to the front desk, Molly was quite pleased with how things turned out.

Upon approaching the registration desk, her sense of all things Slavic were on alert. Without smiling or extending a welcome, the staff person began tapping briskly on an outdated keyboard. Molly watched a series of expressions flash across the man's face. She suspected it was all feigned emotion but, in the span of a few seconds, she witnessed doubt, confusion, confidence, frustration, and finally, disinterest. In a dry and indifferent tone, Molly was informed that there must have been a mistake upon submission of the reservation. Her name was not found in the database. If, however, she was willing to pay a small tax for last-minute accommodations, the hotel could provide her with a room.

Taking it all in stride, Molly paid the small tax—otherwise

known as a bribe—and quite suddenly everything seemed to be put to right. The concierge, as well as the bell boy, and the maid were eager to be of assistance. They were also eager to practice their English with the foreigner. This charmed the educator in Molly, although it went against her grain not to correct their syntax.

Although Slavic languages were similar—they shared the same alphabet and had comparable grammatical structure—English was completely different. And since the Ukrainian staff had graciously conversed with her in Russian, it seemed a bit trite, even to Molly, to reprimand them now as they muddled their prepositional phrases and confused the tense.

The concierge led her to an art deco elevator fashioned from metal filigree. The group entered the enclosure; and when the operator shut the brass accordion-like gate, she could see the cables lift them as the mechanism moaned and creaked its way up to the eighth floor. Escorted by this dedicated team, they eventually reached her room where a stubborn door was coerced to open and Molly was invited to cross the threshold.

The concierge placed the room key directly in the palm of her hand, purposely avoiding the nightstand or dresser. Showing the agility of Russian ice dancers, the maid—who was burdened with linens and towels—and bell boy—who was shouldering her luggage —crossed over the threshold with precision and care. Molly understood these rituals. It was bad luck to place keys directly onto a table, and everyone knew that demons dwelled in the thresholds —at least everyone who knew ancient Slavic superstitions. Thinking her mother would have been proud of her nod to the supernatural, Molly smiled. She then suddenly remembered to have a more dignified expression as she dismissed the staff. Smiling was only appropriate when there was something worth smiling for, and this, she quickly discerned was not the appropriate time.

Finally alone, Molly took a moment to look about the room. It was a good size, clean and well appointed. There was a round oak table with two high back chairs. The lovely quilt upon the bed was intricate and colorful. Molly again thought of her mother and how she would have appreciated the handiwork. There was a personal safe for those travelers who needed to stow away cash, jewelry, or important documents. These things, however, would not be easily accessible as a person would have to get on their hands and knees to operate the combination. It was obvious to Molly that the room's designer didn't think things through.

She never could understand the lack of a simple plan. She was forever creating lists or crafting strategies—her mother said Molly and her father shared the same fault. Judith loved to remind her family of the old Yiddish adage, "Man plans and God laughs." She urged them to loosen up and open up to the Universe. If her mother had her way, Molly would still be dressing up in fairy wings and princess crowns.

As a child, they would go on nature walks, although her mother liked to refer to the outings as enchanting retreats where her daughter could reconnect with nature and her spiritual energy. Off they would go into the woods, dressed in tie-die and gossamer. Her mother would sprinkle "pixie dust" in the air as Molly twirled about and collected wild flowers.

Molly shuddered at the thought of such silliness. She brushed away the memory as if it were her mother's fairy glitter and began quickly unpacking. She had no time to waste. Galina Alexsandrovich was on her way!

CHAPTER TWO

7th of April

Molly had begun unpacking a few of her toiletries when a series of rapid knocks announced the arrival of her anticipated guest. In her eagerness to meet Galina Alexsandrovich, she dropped the duffel bag and rushed to answer the continuous tapping. Molly was ill prepared, however, for the vision of loveliness that stood before her.

Attractive in that fresh-face, girl-next-door way, Molly never went in for the glamour look so popular with the Slavic girls. Standing toe-to-toe with a gorgeous femme fatal, it suddenly occurred to her that she hadn't changed from her brushed denim jeans and simple pink T-shirt. Her unruly curls were haphazardly held back with a headband and her face was Noxzema clean. In contrast, Galina was dressed in a black leather pencil skirt and a silk, leopard print blouse. She sported five-inch stiletto heels. Her eyes were rimmed in black kohl and her pouting lips were lusciously dressed in red gloss. Her raven black hair was the perfect complement to the whole ensemble—sleek and luxurious, not a strand was out of place.

Molly was momentarily tongue tied, but Galina reached over the infamous threshold and proceeded to kiss her on the right cheek, then on the left, and once again on the right.

"My dear Molyia, eh...Mou-lly—eh, I am happy so much you have arrived!"

Standing by the door, with a hand still on the knob, Molly watched as the woman strutted across the room and elegantly took a seat. With a cigarette in one delicately manicured hand, she opened her Louis Vuitton handbag and removed a notebook and pen with the other.

"Come darling. I will call you Malyshka—my little one. I no understandt your name: Moe-li? Come. Sit by me and let us talk. Vhat you hope to findt during stay in Pearl of Black Sea?"

Molly released the door and made her way over to the dinette set. Her nose twitched a bit as she breathed in the heady mixture of Galina's heavy perfume and cigarette. She sneezed—rather unladylike—and proceeded to stumble over her duffle bag. She finally landed onto the chair in a most inelegant fashion. Molly knew she would have to get over her stupefaction of the woman's beauty and femininity, if she wanted to get anything accomplished. *OK! Get over it. You are a professional, for heaven's sake.*

She pulled out her laptop and opened two distinct files—one labeled Russia and the other, Argentina. Squaring her shoulders and looking straight into those kohl-rimmed eyes, Molly—in perfect Russian—began her dissertation on the facts, names, and dates she had so lovingly collected. She held back a sigh when Galina looked appropriately impressed.

"Iz goodt, iz very, very goodt! Now tell me exactly vhat you know about Abramovitz family. Andt please to speak in English. I need practice too much."

Molly acquiesced. She explained that she and her father had been working on the family tree for years. Her mother's branch was fairly complete—this was largely due to the fact that her relatives immigrated to Argentina a good decade after her paternal relatives had arrived. Record keeping had been updated somewhat with the passage of time and that had enabled Molly to track the majority of Judith's side of the family.

Her father's branch required deeper research. The family, being twice as large as her mother's, had spread out across the vast South American country. Many relatives had lost track of one another, having limited mobility and mediocre resources of communication. Molly described how her father reached an impasse in his pursuit of records when, in 1994, the Argentine Israelite Mutual Association building was destroyed by a bomb.

"Eighty-five innocent people were killed in that disaster," she explained. "The AMIA had been the center of Jewish life. It provided religious, social, and educational activities, but it also was the historical center for the community. The terrorist attack decimated untold amounts of documentation relating to Jewish immigration—essentially burying the dead once again."

Because of this tragedy, they—as well as every other genealogy enthusiast—were forever denied access to the historical archives. By discovering his great grandparent's records, her father had hoped to unravel another mystery surrounding the family's name. Tsar Alexander I's edict of 1804 required all Jews living in the

Pale of Settlement to adopt surnames, meaning, of course, that the name *Abramovitz* was only a few generations old.

"When I began helping my father with his research," Molly added, "it became our number one goal to find a death certificate—or other documentation, such as voting records or property deeds, which would have provided further clues to his great-grandfather's story."

Galina understood that tracking down this sort of information would have been tantamount to finding buried treasure. Some documents revealed genealogist gold: names of the deceased's parents, birth place, or occupation. The patriarch was lost to Molly and David; but gladly, they knew his wife's name. It was Malka.

Molly recounted how she and her father had pieced together anecdotes to determine that Baron Maurice Hirsch and the Jewish Colonization Association (J.C.A.) aided the Abramovitz family. Once in Argentina, they were provided with land to farm. But through research, it was discovered that several of Malka's sons had instead become *cuentaniks*, selling fabric and sewing machines. Cuentaniks, Molly explained, was a colloquialism that combined a Spanish word with a Yiddish term. It was the name given to traveling salesman who sold a variety of merchandise in the numerous colonies established by J.C.A.

Many members of the family would eventually grow their cash-on-delivery business and move to Buenos Aires' eleventh district, where they became prosperous merchants in the central neighborhood known as *El Once*. David's father, Ruben, was born in this Jewish enclave—the equivalent to New York's lower east side—in 1927. This last child born to Yosef and Sofia Abramovitz would, in later years, become David and Molly's partner in crime. He enjoyed sharing tales and tried to connect the dots, providing names and dates for his son and granddaughter; but by the time Molly began asking tough questions, Ruben's mind began confusing the data.

There was the question of a mysterious female named Gilberta Saperstein. Was she a blood relation? The name certainly didn't match. She had arrived with the family, but no one could recall her place in the family tree. In addition, records indicated that an Abramovitz child had been born on the ship. The birth had caused quite a ruckus and there had been lingering questions of the child's citizenship. Was he Russian or Argentine? Did he take on the ship's nationality? More importantly: who were his parents? What was his name? The one who would have known these answers—and certainly would have deemed it necessary to share the details—was the matriarch.

Ruben knew his grandmother. Bobe Malka was legendary in the family, but he was just a small boy when she, and her stories, passed away. His grandfather had died in the old country, and there always seemed to be some confusion regarding his name. Was it Shlomo? It may have been Shmuel, Shaul, and Shimon for that matter. Once they translated the names to Spanish, it was difficult to say if his name was Solomon, Samuel, Saul and Simon. The cultural realignment created a veritable mishmash of possibilities. Ruben's memory had melded the conglomeration, and he simply could not recall his grandfather's name with any certainty.

Molly would have continued sharing more details, but the day's travel, the lack of sleep, and Galina's perfume were beginning to take their toll. Her body was sending signals—her pounding head and aching body were telltale signs which she uncharacteristically chose to overlook. However tired, Molly was determined to push through. She had only planned for three days in Odessa and there was no time to waste. Ignoring the warnings of a burgeoning migraine, Molly cautiously sipped from her water bottle and asked Galina if they could continue the conversation en route to the family's home. Unfortunately a headache was not the only thing burgeoning. A full-fledged, Black Sea storm was brewing, so much so, that Galina considered postponing the outing.

Molly practically jumped out of her seat at the thought. After all her careful planning! "Please Galina," she implored. "Couldn't we beat the storm if we leave right away?"

Galina shrugged her delicate shoulders and waived her cigarette about in the air. "Ve have saying in my country: Vithout effort, you cannot pull fish out of pondt."

"So does that means we're going?"

"Iz correct, Malyshka!"

"Why do you refer to me as 'little one'? It's a rather odd nickname for a grown woman, don't you think?"

"It is term of endearment. You have face of little girl, and you are alone in my country. I feel like mama."

Molly laughed. "You are one sexy mama!"

"Being mama does not mean vearing babuska and black shawl, Malyshka. Are you finishedt vith questions?" Galina took a puff of her cigarette. "If ve vait, ve vill needt Noah to buildt ark for us."

The concierge hailed a taxi for the two women, hiding his curiosity towards the mismatched pair. Galina was wrapped in classic black sable from head to toe. A perfumed paisley scarf provided the only relief of color. Molly sported a multicolored puffer jacket. Her mess of curls was unceremoniously stuffed under the faux fur hood. She looked like a frizzy-haired Michelin man. A cab pulled up to the curb. Galina provided instructions and off they went. With rain pouring down in sheets, claps of thunder, and lightning supplying enough drama to satisfy any Russian poet, Molly couldn't help but find the situation ironic.

She had planned every detail, carefully organizing each day. She had envisioned walking into her family's ancestral home with decorum and respect, not frazzled, dripping wet, and fighting off a migraine. She could see her mother's face. She could hear her voice saying once again, "Man plans and God laughs." Molly took another sip of water and whispered, "Not funny, Mom."

Driving along the elegant tree-lined streets, Molly—who had studied the Russian Revival period of design as well as the Byzantine with its mosaics and cupolas—couldn't help but admire the striking estates. She was certainly well prepared for the display of notable architecture, but she was anxious to reach the Abramovitz home and hoped that the neighborhood they were seeking wasn't too far off. As the car stopped in front of an impressive structure, complete with gables and colorful domes, Molly found herself pleasantly surprised.

"This is where my family lived? It's so majestic."

Galina rushed to the massive door eager to get out of the rain. She pulled out an antique skeleton key, turned it in the lock, and pushed the door ajar. With a sweeping motion of her hand, she welcomed her client. "Vhat? You vere expecting shtetl? This is not Anetevka and your great great-grandfather was no Tevye."

Molly took a moment to appreciate the grandeur of her family's estate. Galina was right. She had allowed her imagination to paint in bleak, broad strokes. If most people thought their ancestors were stereotypical characters in a Sholem Aleichem play, that was an innocent, if not an ill-informed, misconception.

That she allowed herself to visualize her family living miserably in a wooden shack at the edge of a fictional village was shameful and immature.

"Vell, don't standt there, come in! Come in!"

The two tentatively crossed the threshold and began looking for a light switch. Galina explained that the house had been updated in the late 1940's; however, she didn't offer any further detail. Molly made note of the year, and because of the history of that time period, didn't push for more information. The years following the Russian Revolution were times of misery and famine under Soviet rule. The subsequent years brought the Nazis and near annihilation of the Jewish community. Her family had thankfully been long gone by World War II. The fact that the house survived the horrors of that era was extraordinary.

If these walls could talk...

Molly assumed Galina didn't want to recall her own family's story. She knew enough not to pursue that line of questioning. Instead, Galina turned the subject back to the economic situation of the Abramovitz family.

"Malyshka, you are student so I remindt you vhat you must already know. After Alexander II, some things improvedt for Jews. As our people vere allowedt to leave Settlement of Pale, those who hadt goodt Russian education vere grantedt greater rights. They vere allowedt to promote to higher academia, vhich ledt to assimilation in Russian society, ah—of course—but not in military. Military didt not vant to associate vith the Jews and so, they couldt not promote to higher strata."

"Yes, yes! That makes sense," Molly said excitedly. "My father and I were never able to track any leads back this far. And to make matters worse, Argentines have an exasperating habit of calling every Jew from Eastern Europe *ruso*. All we knew was that they were from Russia, but of course, that could encompass a wide variety of locations—what with borders changing constantly and governments toppling. Most likely, the family took advantage of the Tsarist legislation in the early 1860's and were allowed to move outside of the Pale," she paused and thought a moment before continuing. "They *would* have been allowed to move if they belonged to the First Merchant Guild...and, if they lived in this house," she stopped to inspect the elegant foyer with its striking woodwork and marble flooring, "they must have belonged to the upper echelons."

"There vere many prominent Jewish families in textile business andt production of grain and sakhar—sugar," Galina offered. "Others vere involvedt in banking andt, of course, many began to enter Russian intelligentsia. Abramovitz family certainly vere Jewish entrepreneurs. Now then, let's begin to explore, yes?"

A regal staircase was the focal point of the room and at the top of the landing, albeit cloudy and cracked, was a magnificent stained-glass window. The two women divided and spread out, curious to see what treasures they could find. The rooms were sparsely furnished, wall hangings and trimmings were torn, decorations or photographs were keenly missing. The few pieces of furniture left behind had been covered with linen, but when exposed, revealed worn and tattered upholstery. In what appeared to be the library, Molly came across a massive oak desk. She was hoping against hope to find letters or family documents, but the drawers were empty. The bookshelves were bare. If there were secrets to be revealed, the house was not in a hurry to share them.

"Malyshka! Are you finishedt downstairs? Please to come to attic so quickly!"

Molly hadn't realized that her companion had moved on without her. Startled, she sprinted up the winding staircase until she came to a landing where she was faced with the option of heading left or right. Her jaw dropped as she crossed in front of an exquisite gold leaf, floor-to-ceiling mirror, but Galina's continual shrieking spurred her on. She veered left and ran past several rooms until coming to an opened door. The entry led to a concealed staircase, short and straight. Molly quickly advanced until coming to the top tread. She found Galina in the attic, surrounded by stacks of grimy books and antique steamer trunks.

"What have you found?" Overcome by the sight that greeted her, Molly stood frozen in the dreaded threshold.

"Malyshka! Look vhere you standt! Come, do not tempt devil. Come!"

"I never dreamed we'd find all of this! I'm a bit surprised that the historical society allowed us access," Molly said, crossing over the tormented space into the relative safety of the attic. She sneezed as a puff of dust greeted her. "I wonder if they realized what treasures would be at our disposal."

"These oldt houses are abandonedt. There iz no money, no interest—not vith political problems ve have today. Historical society iz not interestedt in bits of oldt paper. They are interestedt in new paper—green paper—andt you paidt fee, so all iz goodt!"

"I don't know where to begin." Molly spun around in amazement. "Hopefully, we don't have any unsolicited guests up here," she gurgled, as she began weeding through piles of paper.

"Vhat you mean—*guests*?"

"I mean mice, of course!"

"Ve have saying in my country: Unsolicitedt guest is worse than a Tatar."

At Galina's proclamation, with her manicured hand waving yet another cigarette in the air, Molly let out a peal of laughter. This she immediately regretted. The pounding in her head reminder her that she could run, but she couldn't hide. A migraine was definitely coming, but thankfully, the room was dimly lit. The only source of light came from a single, bare bulb humming away on its last leg of energy. When experiencing her epic migraines, strong light made her nauseous and faint. She was grateful for the darkened room.

The wind was howling now and the light bulb swayed gently as air came through the broken windows. Molly peered through a cracked crystal pane and turned to Galina. She knew that she could spend hours in this room gathering information, and she would be quite content. Galina, however, would be bored to tears —not to mention uncomfortable and hungry. She was a travel advisor, a tourist guide used to visiting museums, theaters, and possibly a synagogue or two. Glamour Girl didn't look like she was cut out for the down and dirty work Molly had in mind. Hoping to convince her companion that she had her best interests at heart, Molly suggested that Galina go home before the storm got any worse.

"Malyshka, vhat you vant from me? I shouldt leave you, by yourself?"

Molly had begun stock piling books and papers. She was willing herself to concentrate on the task at hand. The last thing she needed was Galina looking over her shoulder, waving her cigarette in the air and asking if she was *finishedt* yet.

"Yes, please do go home. I'll be fine. I promise I won't go anywhere else. I'll stay right here, and when I've had enough, I'll take a taxi back to the hotel. Tomorrow we'll have breakfast and you can take me to the Jewish Museum. Does that sound like a good plan?"

"Ve have saying in my country: If you enjoy riding, you must enjoy pulling sleigh."

On another occasion, Molly might have enjoyed the plethora of charming local proverbs, but at this precise moment, her fingers were itching to dig into the buried treasure. Just as her patience began to wane, Galina announced her decision. She was not prepared to do dirty work after all. Three kisses later, Galina sashayed out the front door and Molly was free to *pull sleigh* to her heart's content.

With her eccentric companion gone, Molly went straight to a wooden steamer trunk she had spied upon entering the room. It was extraordinary. Even in the dimmed light, she could see the ornate hardware and embossed trimmings. Gingerly opening the arched dome, she saw several books and recognized the stylized lettering. Her Hebrew skills were not quite up to par, but she sounded the words out as she lifted the books out: Tanakh, Gematria, Kabbalah and—*Tarot*?

"Now that's an interesting combination," she said to an empty room. Used to spending hours on end alone with her studies, Molly—much to her mother's amusement—had developed a habit of speaking out loud. "Are you sure you are speaking to yourself, Molly?" Judith would say, and just to push Molly's buttons, she would add, "Maybe you have an angel by your side who is listening."

Geez! My migraine must really be kicking in. I can't get my mom out of my head. "Enough of that," Molly reprimanded herself, shaking her poor, aching head. "I didn't realize that Jews followed tarot."

While she excelled in Russian history, she reluctantly admitted that her Jewish education was woefully lacking. Although her parents identified with Judaism, they had a unique relationship with the customs and traditions—picking and choosing those attributes that spoke to them personally. They allowed Molly to dictate her level of observance and education; but as a consummate student, she was interested in the history of her faith, not necessarily in the practice. She self-identified as a Jew, but Molly knew she had much to learn.

"When I get back home," she grunted as she moved another stack of books to a side, "I need to take a few courses in Judaic studies."

Molly picked up a book of Gematria and was pleased with herself for recognizing the subject matter. This was in no small part thanks to her mother who felt a connection with the "spiritual" side of Judaism. Anything that allowed for insight into different planes of thought had always fascinated Judith.

Molly's cursory understanding of Gematria's methodology consisted of knowing that numerical values were attached to each letter of the Hebrew alphabet. Calculating the equivalence of each word or phrase could provide immeasurable insight for a student of scripture, as the assumption behind this technique was that *nothing* was coincidental.

Molly and her father thought it to be a charming ideology, and although naturally skeptical, she had grown accustomed to birthday and Chanukah checks made out in increments of eighteen. Eighteen, of course, had the numerical value of the Hebrew word "chai," which also translated to the word "life". Using the Gematria system, the recipient of the monetary gift, was being blessed with a happy, long life.

Setting the book down and choosing an ancient tome of Kabbalah, she began scrolling through its pages. This, too, was one of her mother's favorite subjects, but not because it was suddenly prevalent with movie stars and pop artists. Judith always held that Kabbalah was one of the most grossly misunderstood themes of Judaism, in part because of its doctrines being distorted and used out of context by a modern society. While she yearned to delve deeper into the subject matter and to discuss the realm of the supernatural, Judith recognized that she was ill-prepared to tackle the material. It was not meant for an uneducated public—that was true in ancient times, as well as, the new age. Needless to say, just the *idea* of there being "hidden knowledge" caused lively conversations at the Abramovitz dinner table.

Molly leafed through the book until she came to page marked with a playing card. Decorated in a highly stylized manner, the purple card reminded her of the *fileteo* designs so popular in Argentina. At its center, a large oak tree was surrounded by a variety of esoteric images. Turning the card over, she found another captivating image—a picture of a fairy holding eight spears in her right hand.

"No," she murmured. "She's not a fairy. Wouldn't you know it? She's a queen, complete with a royal crown."

Molly held the card up to the solitary light source in order to read the faint writing around the edges. Her head was pounding, as she began sounding out the words. She had to blink a few times to think through the pain. The light seemed to be getting stronger, and she thought it strange that such a small, worn-out bulb could produce such a powerful stream of energy.

She tried to hold the card up once again, but was blinded by a spark. Closing her eyes made things worse as the room now began to spin. A burst of wind crashed through the fragile cracked window and she heard the bulb shatter. Molly felt an odd sensation in her hand. Her fingers were burning, as if she was holding a flickering match. She felt something tugging on the card, but she couldn't open her eyes to see who, *or what*, was causing the sensation. The last thing that came to her mind before fainting away was Galina's comment about unwanted guests.

CHAPTER THREE

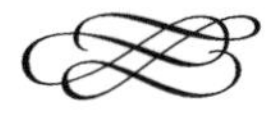

7th of April

Slowly coming around, Molly gently rubbed her temples and blinked a few times to clear her vision. *Man! That was the worst migraine ever!*

"I wonder how long I've been lying here?" she croaked. Her parched throat cried out for water and she tentatively sat up, reaching for her belongings. It was then that Molly heard a soft gasp. "Who's there?" she said, instinctively switching to Russian. "Come on, show yourself."

Remembering the odd sensation of someone tugging at the card she held in her fingers, she suddenly became aware of her precarious situation. Wishing she could find her water bottle, but settling instead for a bronze candlestick she found on the desk, Molly prepared to strike. "I'm ready for you!"

Cautiously looking about the room, she saw the book of Kabbalah. Tossed off to the side was the now-scorched card. As she went to reach for the items, a young boy jumped up from behind the trunk and tried to reclaim the card from her hand. Molly let out a small shout—more from the start, than from fear. She guessed that the boy was about eleven or twelve and seemed to be dressed in a period costume. In her professional estimation, it was quite good.

He must be playing a role. She assumed that Galina had sent the child over to add to the historical drama, but he looked pale and frightened.

Maybe it's his first gig. He seems too shy to do this kind of work. I'll introduce myself and see if I can't get him to say his lines. "Hello," she said, hoping her forced smile was not too frightening. "My name is Molly Abramovitz. I'm here to do some research on my family."

There was silence—crickets even. Molly waited a moment. "My guide, Galina Alexsandrovich, brought me here so that I might look through the family's belongings...you know, things that they left behind when they moved away." She paused and waited for a response, yet the boy was still. "Something odd happened during the storm," she continued. "The window burst and the light went out..."

"Liar!" the boy finally cried out.

"Excuse me?"

"You are a liar! We did not leave anything behind. Why would we? We have not gone. We are still in residence, as you see. This room is my—well—that is not important now. What matters is that you are a liar. I do not know *a Galina Alexsandrovich,* and worst of all, you...YOU APPEARED OUT OF THIN AIR!"

The boy stood shaking and breathless; and in a complete state of amazement, Molly could only return his gaze. An awkward moment passed before they realized that they both now were holding on to the main object of interest—the tarot card.

"It began to burn my fingers," he finally whispered. "I saw a bright light and then...then, you *appeared.*"

"Look little boy," she said gently. "The show is over. Let go of the card. I would like to have a closer look."

At this, the so-called actor took umbrage. "I am not a little boy! I am thirteen years old. I am a bar mitzvah."

I'm so not up for this. Molly rubbed her eyes and let out a deep breath. "Fine. You're a bar mitzvah. You're the big man on campus. So, what's your name?"

"I do not understand your meaning, but my name is Duvid Abramovitz."

"Look, enough is enough! I just told you that *my* name is Abramovitz. You don't have to copy me. What is *your* name? And what are you doing here?"

"But I have just told you. I am Duvid Moiseyevich Abramovitz. My parents are Moishe and Dvora Abramovitz. This is the home of Solomon and Malka Abramovitz, my grandparents."

"You live *here*? With your grandparents?"

"Yes, that is correct," he replied. "My parents, aunts and uncles: Sara, Aaron, Rivka, Avram, Yaacov, Naftali, Ysroel, Efraim, Benjamin, Yosef, and Leah—we all reside here." He spread his arms out wide, trying to encompass as much space as possible. "This room is my secret place. I—I am not supposed to be here. Actually, I am not supposed to be here studying the Kabbalah. I will have to face the consequences now because of *you!*"

"Don't pin your troubles on me. If you're not supposed to be here, that's not my fault."

"You are a thief or a sorceress, I know not. You speak nonsense, but I will let you go, if you promise to leave now and not tell my parents."

Feeling weak, Molly felt her knees give in as she sank back down to the floor.

"Duvid," she said, accepting the Yiddish nickname, "I am not a thief and I'm most certainly am not a sorceress." *Ha! If my mother could hear me now.* "I was given permission to be in this house. And by the way, what you are saying is not funny. I don't know what Galina told you, or how she got the information to you before we did any further research, but this is going to stop now. I don't feel well and I want to go back to the hotel. I need to call a taxi."

Molly attempted to stand up again; when suddenly, the previous conversation replayed in her head. The boy just named the entire Abramovitz family. How did Galina find their names? She must have come to the house before she brought me, Molly thought. She found their names amongst all these papers...*Oh dear Lord!* The boy said his grandparents were Solomon and Malka. Solomon? Malka's husband's name was *Solomon*! That was the name she and her father had been searching for. Could it be true? Had Galina found Yosef's father? The boy's voice brought her attention back to her surroundings.

"Lady Moe-li, I do not understand what you are telling me. If you are not a thief, then why are you here? If you are not a sorceress, how did you enter our home? And why are you dressed in such a manner? You look quite unusual, I must say. I am sorry you are not well. Perhaps I should call my grandmother to assist you. Babe Malka always knows what to do in these situations. She is from the old country and knows many healing methods."

"Bobe Malka is here?" Molly laughed and groaned

simultaneously. "Boy! You're on a roll now! I didn't think you had it in you. Wait! What old country?"

"Excuse me, Lady Moe-li, the word is pronounced *babe* not bobe. And she is from Lithuania. Well, that's not exactly right. She was from there a long time ago. Lady Moe-li, you certainly have a unique way of speaking. Please wait here and do not make a sound. I do not wish to alert the others. I will bring my grandmother to you."

"Okay. Go ahead. Go get your Babe Malka. Go get the matriarch, the queen of the family. I'll just stay right here and wait to wake up from this dream."

Molly didn't know what else to say. *What in God's name was going on?* Galina came very highly recommended, but all this hocus pocus—burning tarot cards, bursting light bulbs, a child actor in short pants—this was not called for. This was not part of the plan. Not knowing how much time she had before the boy and his "grandmother" returned, she began analyzing the situation. She had to get her bearings.

Thankfully, her headache had begun to dissipate and she was able to focus on the items around the room without squinting. She took a turn about the space and came to the conclusion that she must have been moved after she fainted. She *did* remember fainting—although she was embarrassed to admit it. *This can't be the same room.*

The furniture was clean and polished. The beveled crystal panes were intact—no cracks. The room was neither cold, nor dusty and she noticed the stacks of books and piles of documents were missing. There were no signs of the shattered light bulb; however, there were plenty of candlesticks and a gas light fixture.

Molly turned her attention to herself and wondered what had

happened to her belongings. Her purse was gone, which meant that she was missing her passport, wallet, and a few of her personal effects—including her cell phone. She remembered that Duvid thought her clothes were unusual. She acknowledged that she was no fashion plate, usually picking items for their comfort and affordability rather than their appeal. That being said, she didn't think her jeans and T-shirt were so unusual, although she'd be the first to admit that her puffer jacket could be considered a bit odd. It was practical and economical and she was a student, for goodness sake.

Returning her focus to the room—as hard as she tried—she couldn't remember moving or being carried out of the attic. The Victorian estate was quite large, it was practically palatial. How many attics did these homes have, she thought. And then there was the issue of Duvid. He was a cute kid, but that sailor suit! Galina had dressed her little actor to resemble Alexei Nikolaevich of the House of Romanov. *Really, Galina. You could have been a bit more original.*

Thinking of Galina made her a little irritated, to say the least. She must have known about the family all along. She knew about Bobe Malka and that her great-great-grandfather's name was Solomon! She had staged the whole thing—so dramatic—so over the top. So Russian!

Fed up with the theatrics and ready for some answers, Molly decided it was time to leave the estate and head back to the hotel. If Galina had found her family documents, she wanted to see them for herself and not be part of an off-Broadway production of "How Molly met her Ancestors." Just as she went to reach for the door, Duvid came rushing through. He had someone with him. As promised, he brought his grandmother. Molly stepped back and allowed the actors their space.

"See Babe? Here she is. The intruder—she appeared from the thin air. My fingers were burned by the card. And she speaks oddly. And..."

"*Sha*, Duvid," the woman reprimanded. "That will do." She walked slowly across the room and stopped only when her face was just inches away from the intruder. She looked into Molly's eyes and took notice of her mouth, the shape of her nose, the curl of her hair. She took Molly's hands into her own, inspected each finger, and then turned one hand over to examine her palm.

While *Babe Malka* conducted her inspection in silence, Molly took note of the woman, as well. She was impeccably dressed in a period costume. Molly surmised that she was attempting to portray a widow. She wore a mourning dress of black silk moiré. It was trimmed with velvet panels around the edges of the sleeves and decorative braiding around the hem. Molly was a casual dresser personally, but as a historian, she knew authentic period wear.

At first glance, the woman appeared to be in her late sixties. But standing so close, Molly now estimated she might be in her early fifties—possibly her own mother's age. It was hard to tell as she wore no makeup and her salt and pepper hair was severely braided in a crown. Molly suddenly had a flash back. She recalled an old photograph of her great-great-grandmother that had been taken in Buenos Aires. That portrait was of an elegant woman whose pearly, white hair had been fashioned into a braided crown. It was a fitting hairstyle for a woman treated as a queen. Did that image resemble the woman standing before her now? *Get a grip, Molly, and get on with it!*

"So," she began. "You're supposed to be Bobe Malka? It's very nice to meet you. Thank you for the entertainment, but I'm running late and I have to get going..."

"Duvid," Malka interrupted, "tell me again how this young woman came to be in our home. I assume that I do not have to remind you to tell the truth."

"I was...studying, and suddenly realized that it was time for tea. I was going to make my way downstairs, but I wanted to remember where I left off in the chapter. I planned on reading a few more chapters before *Shabbes*—" he paused to see if he would be praised or scolded. Receiving no acknowledgement, he continued. "I found a deck of cards on the desk and chose one to place in the book. As I touched the card, my fingers began to burn. I felt as if someone was pulling it out of my hand. Then there was a sudden burst of light, and I covered my eyes like when we say the *Shema*. When I removed my hand from my eyes, she was there."

"Wow," Molly let out a low whistle. "Very nicely done, Duvid. Bravo!"

David eyed the stranger in astonishment and glanced at his grandmother, waiting for her chastisement. "She *whistled*," he said when no rebuke came.

"Yes, Duvid. I am aware. Please be still, I wish to..."

"Mrs. Kraskov says one should not whistle in the house," the boy interrupted. "It attracts demons."

"Superstitious, are we?" Molly said with growing impatience.

"Young woman, please do be silent for a moment," Malka directed. "You mentioned a card, Duvid. Which one? Show me."

The boy picked up the card and placed it gently in her hand. "Here it is. Do you see? It is burned, just as I said."

Malka examined what remained of the item in question. She

looked at her grandson's fingertips, and again, pulled on Molly's hand to compare the injury.

"What was the last thing you remember saying, young woman, as you held this card in your hands?"

"Fine. I'll play along, *Babe*," Molly replied. "I was reading the words around the image. My Hebrew isn't what it should be, but I can read if I sound it ..."

"And Duvid, what were you doing as you placed the card in the book?"

David shuffled his feet and averted his eyes, ashamed because he had been found out. He knew he wasn't supposed to be in the room, nor was he supposed to be reading these exalted books. He also knew that he couldn't lie to his grandmother, so he spoke the truth. "I, too, was reading the words around the image."

"Well, then. It appears that you both read the incantation of the Queen of Eight Wands at the same time. Magic spells do not offer explanations. It is the way of the spirit world."

Duvid gasped, but bravely confronted his grandmother. "But you don't believe in magic! It is not our way," he cried. "I have heard you say this over and over again. You have explained that just because we do not understand a thing, it does not follow that we must make up silly explanations, nor call it magic."

Malka hemmed and hawed then pinched her grandson's cheek. "Very good, my boychik. This is true, but what do you expect me to tell you? I must not reveal what you are not supposed to know. You are much too young."

"But I am *not* too young," Molly said, finally finding her tongue. "What the hell is going on here?"

"What sort of language is this Miss...? What is your name, and what, may I ask, do you call this form of attire?"

Molly felt as if she were in the principal's office in elementary school. Gone was her bravado, but she was prepared to answer the woman's questions, just as long as she could get some answers herself.

"I'm Molly Abramovitz. I was recently in Moscow attending a conference on the history of Imperial Russia for my graduate program. I've come to Odessa to research my family genealogy. As I have already explained to the boy, my guide, Galina Alexsandrovich brought me here—to my family's last known residence—and then, very conveniently left me alone so that I could enjoy this theatrical performance. I am now ready to go back to my hotel. I need to call Galina."

Malka waved her hand about in the air as if she were wiping away Molly's speech. "Mou-llye? Mau-li? What sort of name is this? Are you idishke? Are you a scullery maid or a chimney sweep that you wear men's clothing?"

"Am I idishke?" she repeated. "Yes, I am Jewish. To answer your other, rather rude, question, I am not a scullery maid or a chimney sweep; although, I have recently been called worse," she said, glaring at the boy. "I'll have you know that I have a Bachelor of Science in Education and am working on my Master's degree on Imperial Russian History. And my name is Molly, not Mou-llye. And my headache is returning, thank you very much."

"Bring your grandmother a chair, Duvidik," bade Malka, as she continued her interview. "Young lady, you say you a Jewish. What is your given name? For whom were you named when you were blessed as an infant?"

Molly looked at the woman and noticed that her complexion had suddenly become slightly green. She couldn't blame her, as she was feeling quite nauseous herself. "My given name is Molly;

but if you are referring to my *B'rit Bat,* I was blessed with a Hebrew name in honor of my great-great-grandmother."

"Yes?"

"I was named Malka."

"*Azoy*?" said the woman. "And tell me, malyshka, what do you know of your father's people?"

"My father is the son of Ruben Abramovitz," she sighed as she began her recitation. "His grandfather was Yosef. They lived here in Odessa—in this very house." Molly provided what little information she had of the other relatives; and then, not waiting for a chair for herself, plopped down on the floor and crossed her legs like a kindergartener. *I guess it's true. I am a malyshka. I'm a mess—that's what I really am.*

"Very impressive. You are able to account for so many in your family tree. This is rather unusual for someone as young as yourself, is it not?"

"As I mentioned earlier, I am a genealogist and a historian. That's what I do. The stories of my ancestors have always fascinated me. I am in awe of their accomplishments; and although I'd never admit it to my mother, I feel a strange spiritual connection with them." Molly couldn't believe she was sharing these feelings with complete strangers. But before she could stop herself, she revealed a deeper secret. "It's as if they are crying out to me: Don't forget us."

Malka examined the tarot card again. She asked to see the book Duvid had been reading and she reviewed several passages, turning the pages back and forth, comparing sections and making mental notes. She looked deeply into Molly's eyes and breathed in sharply.

"Malyshka, you will stay with the family until we can replace this card. It is the only way you can return to your own time. You and Duvid have opened up a space in time that allowed you to travel here...to your family's home."

"Now wait just a minute!" Molly cried out. "You expect me to believe that I've entered some sort of worm hole? I'm an educated, modern woman. My mother might go for this sort of thing, but not me. You've put on a great show, and you look the part—everything's great, but it's time for me to get back to my schedule."

"My dear, if you are an educated woman than you must know that unexplainable does not mean inexplicable. And although I am not a modern woman in your eyes, my father was ahead of the times and he saw fit to educate his only child. He was my teacher, my rabbi. We studied many books and philosophies. Do you know the Sefer Yetziroh? It is an important book in the world of Jewish mysticism."

"Are you telling me that you believe in magic—that you use Tarot?"

"I believe that if a person is dealing with some difficulty, "magic" presents itself by illuminating a path for the troubled soul. I believe that our innermost thoughts and desires are mirrored in the tarot. It is then up to us to decide how to interpret the meaning of the cards."

"Are you saying that Duvid and I picked up this card in particular because our innermost thoughts called us to it? *Please...*"

"Let me share with you what this specific card represents," Malka suggested. "You are free to decide for yourself, to reason and deduce, if it pertains to you."

Molly nodded her head, silently acquiescing.

"The Eight of Wands contains a high level of energy and movement. It is meant to assist you, to propel you forward towards a goal, especially when one feels conflicted or less than optimistic. The number Eight represents structure and the wands embody energy. Thus, the structure of the numerical value creates a channel through which the energy may flow. I believe you called it a "worm hole"—heaven forbid! In any case, this card foretells of travel—a whirlwind trip, a life-altering experience. Do you understand my meaning? You not only had a card of significant numerical value, but one containing the image of the Queen of the Tree of Life. What say you now?"

"I am speechless," Molly murmured. "How can this be?"

"Just because you do not understand it, does not mean it is not so," a whisper came from a corner of the room.

"Yes—thank you, Duvid," Molly attempted to smile at the boy. "To be quite honest, I had read some material of the Baal Shem Tov and the early Hasidic movement. I know that by the 1830's, the majority of Jews in Ukraine, Galicia, and central Poland were Hasidic and leaned towards mysticism. But I never delved deeper into Kabbalah and the like because my studies pertained to Russian history in general. My father, David..."

Molly paused for a moment and looked at the young boy staring at her. David Abramovitz. "Ah—as I was saying, my father is an intellectual. He was my teacher and partner in history and genealogical studies. My mother leans towards the spiritual world, but Dad and I crave facts and figures. We seek solid evidence—things that are black and white. I desire constancy. I seek stability."

"My dear, I understand this yearning for predictability and stability. My father was raised in Lithuania and was surrounded by great minds, great rabbis. He was immersed in the academic culture. Neither his predecessors nor his colleagues were in favor of the Kabbalistic movement, but my father was part of a group of men that were free thinkers. They found that it was not necessary to completely alienate one form of Judaism from another.

In the same manner that he believed it worthy to instruct his daughter in Torah and Talmud, he wished to impart the spiritual aspect as well. There is no form of Judaism which does not believe in daily miracles. Jewish life has always related to mysticism in some fashion and the *Ruach Hakodesh*, the Holy Spirit."

Molly tried to absorb what she was hearing, but it was all too much. Her throat was clenching; yet somehow, she managed one last question. "Bobe Malka?

"Yes, my dear?"

"What year is this?"

"By our Hebrew calendar," the woman murmured, "it is the year 5660. In modern terms, my *sheine meidelach*, take a look and see for yourself."

Anxious and disturbed, Molly turned to look at the Gregorian calendar above the desk. There it was, in black and white: April 7, 1900.

CHAPTER FOUR

7th of April

Molly stared at the date and, for a brief moment, saw herself walking in the fields with her mother. It was April, the first few days of spring. They were picking daisies and her mother was singing some Beatles song:

Little darling, the smiles returning to the faces
Little darling, it seems like years since it's been here
Here comes the sun, here comes the sun
And I say it's alright.

"It's definitely not alright," she murmured.

"Lady Moe-li, are you not feeling well?"

"I am not a "lady," Duvid. I'm just a girl from California—a girl who lives in the year 2015," Molly groaned and let her head sink into her hands. When she was able to find her voice again, she broached the question that had to be asked. "Are you truly advising me to stay with you until we find a replacement for this card? I can't do that. It is out of the question."

"Very well, Moe-li. What do you suggest?"

"I could...I will call..." She surprised herself. She was actually at a loss. There was no logical solution for this predicament. "I am of no use in these situations," Molly admitted. "I can't deal with spontaneous issues. I need *a plan.* I need to know what steps to take. I need to know what is expected of me."

"I see you take after your Zeide Solomon," said Malka, elegantly hiding a chuckle behind an embroidered handkerchief. "Very well, this is what I propose. To begin with, you will have to meet the family. We will say that you are visiting from Lvov. You shall be the daughter of one of our business associates. That will suit, I believe. We will explain your...*your peculiarities* to the family as stemming from your being a Galitsyaner."

"I'm sorry—what?"

"Although such nonsense may be construed as *Lashon Hara*, there may be some truth to the matter—you see, my dear, we are Litvaks. We came from Lithuania many years ago. And as such, we carry such as labels as unemotional, analytical, and learned. By contrast, those from Polish regions are categorized as being warmhearted, folksy, or even a bit eccentric. Because we are from different localities, we have differences in our food. We Litvaks prepare our varenyky and gefilte fish savory. The Polishe prefer sweet. In other words, if you do or say something *unique,* I will simply say it is your Galitsyaner ways."

"Oh, that's just great. I'm the quirky foreigner from the twenty-first century."

"My dear, this is exactly my point. *Quirky foreigner*, indeed. Now then, you will need the appropriate clothing. We will see what Leah has in her wardrobe that may suit. I would rather not involve my youngest daughter, but we do not have a choice in the matter. There will be too many opportunities for you to misstep or misspeak, and Duvid cannot be your constant companion. That simply will not do. I will have to insist that she keep your confidences. Our Leah can be a bit of a *yenta*, at times."

"She sounds lovely."

"She is your great-grand aunt, my dear. You will meet the rest of the family tonight at Shabbes dinner. Are you prepared? Are you ready to meet your great-grandfather and all his siblings?"

"I came to Odessa to find birth certificates, marriage contracts and old photographs. Instead, I'm going to sit down to Shabbes dinner and ask my great-grandfather—who is currently four years my junior, by the way—to pass the *challah*," Molly laughed, as the sarcasm dripped from lips. "Why wouldn't I be prepared?"

Turning her attention to her grandson, the disciplinarian now came through. Malka was not a petite, sweet old lady. She was statuesque, and at this moment, she was rather intimidating.

"Duvid, I will have your word as a gentleman of this household that you will not betray the truth of today's occurrences."

"Yes, of course, Babe." The boy bowed in deference.

"And do not believe for one moment that I have forgotten what you were doing here in the first place. I do not wish to see you sneaking about the house. With your grandfather gone, and your father and uncles busy with politics and business, no one is providing guidance. I will see to it that you are properly instructed, and given access to only that which I deem appropriate for your age and comprehension."

"Thank you, Babe, but I am not a child. I am a bar mitzvah..."

"I know exactly who and what you are, silly boy, but you will adhere to my decision. Nothing is forbidden to you, only postponed. Knowledge is of no use if not used in its proper context. And now, Moe-li, allow me to escort you to your chamber. You will rest before dinner. I will bring you something for your headache, my dear. You've had quite a time of it, haven't you?"

"I would appreciate a glass of water and some acetaminophen," Molly said, rubbing her temples. "The highest potency you have, if you please."

"I believe I have some Tilia blossoms left over from when Duvid took ill last winter. I will make a nice strong cup of tea, and you will recover quite nicely in no time at all."

"Blossoms?"

"Yes, my dear, from the Tilia tree, but perhaps you are familiar with the vernacular term—the Linden tree? It is quite soothing. It will calm your mind and ease the tensions. This will allow you to sleep." Malka reached for Molly's arm and led her to the door. "Shall we go?"

Up until that moment, Molly hadn't considered what she would find upon entering the hallway. Opening the door and crossing the threshold would confirm she was truly in another world—in another place in time. Somehow, she would have to muster up the courage and face the unknown. Like it or not, she was no longer an American tourist or a genealogical scholar. She was a guest from Lvov in 1900.

It turned out that crossing the dreaded threshold was not as difficult as Molly expected. Once she accepted her current predicament and allowed for events to take their natural course, she found that she had more than enough courage...at least to reach her bedroom. Bobe Malka walked silently along her side.

The only thing to be heard was the rustling of her silk skirt. They reached the third floor, turned down the hall, and stopped at the second door.

"The family is situated in the east wing on the floor below, my dear. I think it best that you remain on this level," she said. "I do hope you will find our guest accommodations pleasing."

Molly walked in and immediately felt as if she had stepped into a fairytale. The room was simply lovely. The walls were covered in blue and white chintz with matching drapes and upholstery, while a thick carpet covered the floor. The fabrics and design made the space plush and welcoming. A dressing screen was placed in the corner. The high back bed had decorative carving and delicate gold incising on the posts and panels. Molly noted the matching dresser, washstand, and vanity. The bed was so inviting, she couldn't resist lying down.

"Yes, Moe-li, rest now. I suppose the tea will not be necessary after all. I will return with a proper gown for dinner. We will worry about the rest of your wardrobe tomorrow..." Malka saw that her charge had already fallen asleep. She walked to the bed, tucked an embroidered shawl around the girl's shoulders and kissed her great-great-grandchild's cheek ever so lightly. "Now to deal with Leah," she said, closing the door behind her.

Her capricious daughter was quite the charmer, but Leah could often times be quite rebellious. It would be wiser not to involve the girl, Malka thought, but she could not manage without her help. She knocked twice on her daughter's door and entered without waiting for a response. She found her daughter sprawled across the bed, her face buried in book. The girl didn't notice her mother for a moment or two. Malka stood quietly by her side, amused at her daughter's deep concentration.

"It is unfortunate that you are not able to dedicate yourself to your studies as well as you do that romance novel, my dear."

"Matushka! Forgive me. I did not hear you come in."

"I am quite aware of that fact, Leah. Now, please put the book down for a moment. I have something to discuss with you and it is of the utmost importance. I will have your word of honor that you will follow my instructions to the letter," Malka paused and ominously lowered her voice. "There will be severe consequences if you fail me in this. Do I make myself clear?"

The poor girl had been caught completely unaware. Leah tried to remember a litany of possible situations that might have vexed her mother, but nothing in particular came to mind.

"What is it, Mama? What have I done?"

"Be still, you foolish child. For once, you have not caused the problem. Listen carefully now. I do not have time to repeat myself..."

For the next twenty minutes, Malka explained the extraordinary situation to her daughter, all the while thinking the girl was too unpredictable to be trusted. Upon completing her soliloquy, Malka carefully examined her daughter's face. Expecting to see fear or amazement, or even excitement at the possibility of causing mischief, Malka only saw determination and gratitude.

"It is quite astonishing, is it not?" the girl said. "Thank you for placing your trust in me, Mama. I will do my utmost to be of assistance. When might I meet our guest?"

"We shall allow her to rest for another quarter of an hour.

Afterwards, I will introduce you to your great-grandniece. In the meantime, there is the question of her wardrobe. The poor dear cannot be seen in her current attire."

With that, mother and daughter—united in their efforts—conspired to put together several suitable ensembles. There was no telling how long Molly would be staying with them. If necessary, they would have to call in the *modiste*, but Malka hoped that it wouldn't come to that. She needed to see the girl safely back home. The longer she stayed, the more precarious the situation for all involved.

Alone in a strange room, Molly opened her eyes and gulped—hard. It was not a dream. It was 1900, and she was napping in her great-great-grandparents' home. How was she going to explain this to her family? To Michael?

Michael's send off at the airport had been terse and uncharacteristically blunt. He had accused her of putting off his marriage proposal because she was not a fan of his adventurous nature, yet there she was—going off on an adventure of her own. And that was the point, he said. It was *her* adventure and she felt in control. The idea that she was in control of anything was ludicrous. We can control nothing, but our own reactions, he exclaimed. The insatiable need for planning and organizing was ruling her life. Sometimes, a person just needed to let go of the reins and trust that they were capable of handling whatever came their way. *Well, Michael, I've let go of the reins now. This was certainly not part of my plan!*

There were two soft taps on the door. Molly sat up in bed,

unsure of how to respond. What if it were a chamber maid or a family member? She wasn't prepared for that encounter. She hadn't had a chance to organize her thoughts. Bobe Malka walked in and was followed by a young woman—a teenager to be exact. Molly thought she recognized the girl. *I must have seen a photograph of this girl as a grown woman.*

"I hope you have had a pleasant rest, my dear," said the elder woman.

"Yes, thank you," Molly replied. "The bed is very comfortable and the room—the room is breathtaking. It reminds me of Tonya's bedroom from *Doctor Zhivago.*"

"Yes, my dear—well—I have brought someone with me, as you can see. I wish to present my daughter, Leah Solomonovna. I have explained the situation; there is no need to be uneasy."

Molly stood, uncertain of the proper protocol of meeting one's great-grandaunt. Leah solved the problem by performing a small curtsy, and then coming full speed to receive her enchanting visitor with a hug and three kisses.

"I am so very pleased to meet you Moe-li. This is so very exciting. Who is Doctor Zhivago? Is he your intended? How romantic! I am very happy that you are here. What an adventure! Nothing ever has happened like this before! It's so dull at home, and the boys are forever busy with politics and the women are..."

"That will do, Leah. A modicum of decorum, daughter." Malka patted the girl's hand and turned to her guest in determination. "Now then. We have selected a gown that will do for tonight, and there are several ensembles from which to choose for the next few days. We might have to call Larisa, the modiste, but we will worry about that next week."

"Next week? How long do you expect me to be here? Bobe Malka, I have a plane to catch in three days!"

"The word is pronounced *babe*," Leah eagerly interjected. "And what is a plane?"

"Well, I pronounce it *bobe*," Molly snapped. "That's how my Argentine grandparents taught me. And a plane is..."

"Moe-li, I beseech you—do not explain any further. It is dangerous for us to know these things, my dear. You must not divulge information of the future—about our future."

"Of course!" Molly let out a nervous laugh. "I'm in a Star Trek episode and am bound by the Prime Directive. How foolish of me to have forgotten."

"Mama, what is she talking about?"

"It's a television show my parents and I used to watch. Dad liked to pretend he was Mr. Spock and..."

"Malkale, please!"

Hearing the familiar term of endearment cut her to the quick. "Please don't call me that. My name is Molly. Malka is *your* name."

"As you wish, my dear, but we cannot continue calling you Moe-li. It will cause too many questions, and we need you to blend in as much as possible. We shall call you Marina, if you agree. And please, you must be very careful with what you say—even to me. I must insist. While you are here—and I do not know how long that might be—you must not disclose any further information about the future."

"Yes, of course. I wasn't thinking," she replied, regretting her childish outburst. "I'll be careful."

"May I help you dress—Marina?" Leah asked, holding up a gown for her inspection.

"I haven't needed help to dress in a long time," she grinned, "but I think I may have to take you up on the offer. Thank you, Leah."

The women were now on a mission, and Molly had no idea what was in store. A copper tub was brought in by two servants. They were followed by four chamber maids, each with two buckets of hot water in tow. Lavender soap and towels were set on the vanity. Molly began removing her T-shirt anxious for a long, soothing soak when Leah shrieked.

"The dressing screen, Moe-li!"

Malka hushed the girl and directed poor Molly to undress behind the screen. The Victorian sensibilities of her family hadn't quite settled in just yet. Once again, Malka reminded her daughter to moderate her tone, and cautioned both to remember to use the appropriate name.

"We must proceed with care. After all, we have just made your acquaintance, malyshka. We should not have any difficulty in saying Marina over such a name as I never heard: Moe-li."

Attempting to be modest while bathing was quite the undertaking, but once done, Leah began working with Molly's mop of chestnut curls. Although she tried to explain that nothing could be done to tame the tousled mass, Leah worked her own special magic and was quite pleased with the results. Molly was shocked that her hair was brought under control, without any of the modern paraphernalia she had stored under her bathroom sink. In fact, she was about to tell Leah about her blow dryer with the diffuser attachment, her ceramic flat iron, the various bottles of hair goop, but she remembered her promise and decided it was better to keep her mouth shut.

Malka began laying out a variety of items on the bed. She

motioned for Molly to approach. "Here you are, my dear. Take these things behind the dressing screen and let us know when you need assistance."

"Yes, but are all these things really necessary?" Molly picked up something flimsy and recognized that they were underwear—bloomers, in fact. They were made of linen and split in the middle. Each leg was finished separately with lace and joined together with a silk draw string at the waist.

"Well, yes—of course. We brought you fresh drawers and these items as well: a chemise, a corset, and corset-cover to protect the gown from the corset, a petticoat and a small bustle pad. But you might not need the bustle," Leah added with a giggle. "Your derriere and hips will fill the dress quite nicely!"

"That is quite enough," Malka sighed.

As the two women played out their roles of couturier and seamstress—poking, pulling, and prodding—a small tear appeared at the cusp of the sleeve. Leah immediately set out to repair the opening before any further damage occurred. As she expertly threaded the needle, Leah handed Molly a short strand from the spool.

"Here you are, Marina."

"What is this for?"

"Don't be silly. Chew on the thread while I stitch the tear."

Bewildered, Molly couldn't help but ask. "Uh—why do I need to chew on the thread?"

"Mir zollen nit farnayen der saychel," Bobe Malka said with a chuckle.

"I'm sorry, but I don't understand Yiddish."

"Then allow me to translate," said Leah. "You mustn't allow someone to sew on your person. It tempts the demons."

"What?"

"Everyone knows a shroud is sown around a corpse—the demons might think you are already dead. We mustn't tempt fate!" Leah said quite seriously and proceeded to spit lightly—three times over her shoulder. "The action of chewing shows them that you are very much alive."

"Oh please! Leah, you can't believe that foolishness."

"There. I am finished," she said, snipping away at the tiny remnants. "It is not foolishness. Tell her Mama."

"My dear, there is a saying—" Malka stopped for a moment and smiled at her visitor. "It was written in *Sefer Hasidim*, the 13th century book of the Pious. You therefore must understand, I take it very seriously. 'One should not believe in superstitions, but it is best to be heedful of them.'"

Molly didn't know whether to laugh or cry. She couldn't help but think of her mother, and how she would be enjoying the entire experience. One last tug from a persistent Leah and Molly was finally allowed to look in the mirror. Stunned, she gasped at her reflection.

Molly recognized the style; she had seen one quite similar in the museum. It had belonged to the Empress Alexandra Fyodorovna. The docent had provided a fine description of the gown, and looking in the mirror, she felt like she was wearing a carbon copy of the princess-cut satin sheath. She noted that the torch sleeves were almost identical to the original design, and the fitted bodice outlined a shape she rarely exposed.

Molly had never seen such attention to detail. It had to have taken hours upon hours to embroider each bead and sequin onto the pink chiffon overlay. How am I going to walk in this?

Staring in the mirror, she wondered how best to manage the

flared skirt and train. *I won't make it down the stairs. I'll fall flat on my face!*

"Oh, Mama! She looks lovely."

"Yes, Leah, you chose well. The gown suits your coloring, Marina. The pink compliments your skin tone and the sapphire of your eyes. It is very becoming, indeed."

"I'm looking in the mirror, but I have no idea who is staring back at me. I've never looked like this before. I've never worn anything as luxurious as this gown, not even to prom."

"What is *prom*, Marina?"

"Oh—um, it is something like a debutante ball," Molly quickly added, peering at Bobe Malka under her eyelashes.

"You had a coming-out ball?" Leah shrieked. "You danced with men?".

Malka closed her eyes and waited to hear what she knew was coming.

"I should be attending my debutante ball next season for my eighteenth birthday, but it is not our way. Men and women are dancing together in our community, but Mama won't allow it because Avram believes it is inappropriate. *Avram* thinks everything is inappropriate. Oh Moe-li—ah—Marina, it would be lovely if you and I could attend a ball together. You, in pink, and I in my favorite emerald-green, we would have our pick of the gentleman!"

"Yes, Leah, it would lovely—I am sure. But I don't know the current dance steps; and more importantly, I hope to be home long before the next season. And, of course, you must consider Avram's opinion."

"The world is changing, Marina," Leah said with a childish stomp of her foot. "Avram needs to pay attention."

"Ah—excuse me," Molly paused to think, "who *exactly* is Avram?"

"He is my third son, after Moishe and Aaron," Malka answered, satisfying Molly's curiosity. "I have to admit. Avram is quite an old soul. He was named for his great-great-grandfather—a man of tremendous knowledge. He had a heart of gold, but *oy*! What a temper! If truth be told, my brilliant son storms about the house, acting as if he were the reincarnation of that curmudgeon."

The three women shared a laugh at poor Avram's expense. Malka had expertly smoothed things over and brought Leah's outburst to an end. Realizing the time, she now ushered Leah out of the room, informing Molly that they would return shortly after attending to their own toilette. Leah blurted out one last instruction as she skirted out the door—very unladylike to be sure.

"Whatever you do, do not sit down!"

Molly hearkened to the warning, not wanting to crease the borrowed gown. She was too excited to sit in any case. Avram was named for his great-great-grandfather! Here was another piece of the puzzle. Mentally adding up figures, Molly put Avram's current age at about thirty. Calculating the number of years in between generations, she put great-great-grandfather Avram's birthdate around the late 1760's. The imperial directive for Jews to assume legal surnames would have affected his children; therefore, Molly deduced that her surname, Abramovitz, stemmed from this particular cantankerous, yet beloved, ancestor.

It seemed an eternity, but finally, Bobe Malka came to Molly's door. Her hostess had changed her gown, still in unrelieved black; however, the bodice was handsomely trimmed in organza and black pearl beads with satin rosettes. A light shawl shimmered across her shoulders. Seeing her again in black reinforced the point that her great-great-grandmother was in mourning. Molly and her father were never able to find out the reason or the date of her husband's death. Molly was hesitant to bring up the topic, but who knew how long she would be among the family? She decided she should try to get as many details as possible.

"You look very nice," she began, "but... ah, I have a question. Is it alright to ask about my great-great-grandfather?"

"Oh bless you my dear, yes—of course. Your Zeide Solomon has been gone for several years now. It was Typhus that took my beloved. Leah had just turned twelve. We were afraid that the children would contact the disease, but we were spared that tragedy. *Baruch Hashem.*"

"But you still are in mourning? After five years? Wouldn't you prefer to wear something more—I don't know...cheerful? You are still young."

"I am fifty-two years old and a mother of twelve children. I had a good life with my husband. We were a good match. I am content, my dear. I have no desire to look differently. Now you, on the other hand, look very charming indeed. And so it should be."

"May I ask another question?" Here was the opportunity of a lifetime—this was a genealogist's dream come true.

"You may ask any manner of question, my dear."

Molly thought how she could phrase her question without sounding heartless. The burial society had informed her that various local cemeteries had been ransacked, but that was in the future. The destruction hadn't occurred yet. Finding there was not an easy way to ask, she simply blurted out her request.

"I was wondering where he was buried. Could we visit his gravesite?"

"It is that important for you, malyshka?" said Malka, her voice heavy with emotion.

Suddenly moved by the intimate moment, Molly put aside her need to investigate—to hunt for a death certificate or look for clues on the tombstone. "Yes, I would like to honor his memory," she replied. "My father would want me to place a stone on his great grandfather's tomb."

A poignant pause followed as Molly contemplated her thoughts. "A small stone may seem meaningless in the grand scheme of time and space. But that stone represents our love of family and respect for the deceased. I may not be here for long, but that stone will not wither away like some flower."

Malka squared her shoulders and stood at her full height. "Very well, I will see to it. I believe my Solomon would be very pleased, indeed." She dabbed away a runaway tear. "And now, my dear, let us meet the family. They will be waiting dinner. I informed our cook, Mrs. Kraskov, that we had a guest and asked that another setting be placed beside me. Shall we go?"

CHAPTER FIVE

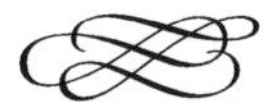

7th of April

As they descended the grand staircase, Molly's stomach began twisting and she was finding it difficult to breath.

"Regulate your breath, my dear. You will soon faint away otherwise. Are you stays too tight?"

Molly managed a nervous laugh. "My stays?" *Dear Lord! I'm a character in a Jane Austen novel!* "No, it's not this wretched corset. It's a bad case of nerves. I just can't wrap my head around what has happened to me and I'm just not a spur-of-the-moment type of girl."

Leah came bouncing out of her room at that moment and joined the two women.

"Do we not make a lovely trio?"

She twirled around to show off the ruffles in her skirt and completed a charming curtsy. Her display of enthusiasm helped calm Molly's nerves. As they reached the double doors to the dining room, Molly noticed the Shabbat candles were already lit.

"Someone has already said the blessing for the candles...?"

"Why yes, of course. Look at the time, my dear. Shabbes does not wait. We welcome the Shabbes Queen at the appropriate time, and now we will break bread together and say the *hamotzi*."

"Oh. I suppose that's the proper way. We—at home, that is—we don't always light the candles on Friday night. We are not always able to gather at the same time. Sometimes, we wait until Dad returns from the university. We are—um, we are not—uh, we are not religious."

"Malyshka, do not concern yourself. I am not so pious as to criticize your ways. We, in this household, are of many minds. Some of my children are traditional and follow the ancient rituals. Some of the younger ones lean towards a more modern interpretation, however, the schedule for lighting the candles is one tradition I hold very dear. Since I was not present at the appointed time, my daughters, Sara or Rivka, would have said the *bracha*."

"But isn't it disrespectful to light the candles if the family is not gathered together? Shouldn't one wait for the head of the household?" Molly asked with sincere curiosity.

"In my mind, the mitzvah of reciting the candle blessings is the act of uniting with the energy of untold households. Imagine it—women throughout this land and across the world at the appointed time are lighting the candles, praising Hashem, thanking Hashem...all praying for peace at the same time. Think of the power created by those women! It would not be the same, if each one lit her candles at whichever time was convenient. Do you not agree?"

"I will have to think on it and let you know," Molly said with a bit of a grin. "I assumed that you might not approve of my family's ways. That wasn't fair. I prejudged. I am pleased to see that, at least, *you* have an opened mind."

"My father would say this is how it should be. Each one of us finds his or her own path. If I force my ways on you, you would not look upon the Lord with love, but with fear. The Hasidim are very different than the Misnagdim, but we are *all* children of Hashem."

"Bobe, I don't know if most people would agree with you."

"My dear, I only need to concern myself with my own conscience."

Molly was not one to take these sort of conversations lightly. She had to sit with them and mull things over. Comparing, justifying, rationalizing—but, there was no time. Without noticing, she had entered the dining room by Bobe Malka's side and was completely unaware of the many curious eyes upon the pair.

"*Gut Shabbes* to all," the matriarch announced. "I am dreadfully sorry we are late. Our guest just arrived this afternoon and her journey has been quite vexing, to say the least. To make matters worse, the poor dear has been separated from her equipage. Leah was able to come to her aid for this evening. Baruch Hashem."

Malka stood at the head of the table and inspected her large family, mentally assessing who might cause trouble and who would prove to be gracious. "My dears, allow me to present Miss Marina. She is visiting from Lvov and will be with us for a short time while her papa is traveling. He is in the textile market and is a business associate of ours."

"Gut Shabbes."

"Good evening, Miss Marina."

"Welcome Miss Marina."

The salutations came from one and all around the grand dining room table. One of Malka's sons came to greet his mother and her guest. He executed a gallant bow and then turned to his mother with a curious look about his face.

"Thank you, Mama, for joining us for our Shabbes meal—and with an unexpected guest, no less. Miss Marina from Lvov? Is that correct?"

"Yes, Avram," Malka sighed, "as I intimated a moment ago."

"Aha, quite so. Miss Marina...?"

Molly wasn't sure what he wanted her to say. She waited for Bobe Malka to speak, but she the matriarch only gave her a regal nod and proceeded to take her seat. With a wave of her hand, she indicated that all should do the same. A footman held out a chair for Molly. Being unaccustomed to the chivalry—let alone to the yards of material of the delicate evening gown—Molly took the offered seat rather clumsily much to her mortification.

Clearing his throat, Avram caught his jittery guest off guard. "Miss Marina," he began, "what is your family name, if one may be so bold as to enquire?"

Again, Molly waited for aid from her hostess but none came from that quarter. She had to come with up with something, and so she did.

"Davidovich."

Malka smiled at the response.

"And your father is...?" Avram persisted.

"David."

"David Davidovich? I don't believe I know the gentleman. Mama, tell us again. How exactly are we acquainted?"

"Avram, as you just so eloquently reminded me, it is Shabbes. Mrs. Kraskov is holding our dinner. May we begin please?"

"Yes, of course Mama. After all, we may converse throughout the meal." And with that, Avram found his seat next to his wife, Bluma—a pale and sullen woman.

Duvid, looking quite grown up in his blue velvet suit, sat alongside his parents and beamed at Molly from across the table. She was practically jumping out of her skin with excitement as his uncles, Ysroel, Benjamin, Efraim and Yosef, introduced themselves without waiting for their mother's interference. Bobe Malka completed the round by presenting her remaining children.

Naftali and Yaacov sat by Avram and spoke amongst themselves. They did spare her a glance and a brief nod, but no more than absolutely necessary. By the look of their clothing, the *peyot* and *tzizit*, Molly knew that these sons were the traditionalists that Bobe Malka mentioned earlier. That left Moishe and his twin Aaron, Rivka, and Sara, the eldest. There were of course, an assortment of husbands and wives; their youngsters already upstairs in the nursery. Only Duvid was allowed to dine with the adults as he was now a bar mitzvah.

"We shall all be well acquainted in a day or two," said Malka. "Marina, my dear, please feel quite at home."

The blessing over the bread was recited and the soup was served. Molly took the opportunity to look about at her surroundings. Without a doubt, her family was of the upper echelons of society. The elegant dining room seemed to be connected to the kitchen by way of a butler's pantry. Off to the side, Molly could see another very pretty room which she assumed was the drawing room. The ladies would surely adjourn there after the meal. She knew this was quite customary, not from history books, but rather from her mother's *big skirt* movies, as Molly dubbed them years ago. She almost laughed aloud when she realized, yet again, that she was smack in the middle of one of her mother's period dramas.

The room was magnificent with dark woods, luxurious fabrics, and shimmering candles that played off the crystal chandelier and the ladies jewelry. Molly was in awe of her opulent surroundings. Yet, she was not quite at ease. All this wealth and extravagance... how did the family rise to success during the reigns of such royals as Nicholas and Alexander? Molly didn't know how they managed to reach this social strata, but she knew history. She knew what was coming and for that reason, the ostentatious lifestyle of her family filled her with dread.

To make matters worse, as she tried to daintily sip her soup, she noticed that Ysroel, Benjamin, and Efraim were vying for her attention. Any excuse they could find to approach her side of the table was up for grabs. Benjamin nearly toppled his chair when he leapt up to refill his mother's wine glass. Ysroel was a bit more gallant, but he too rushed to his mother's side when her shawl dropped to the floor. Efraim made a production of bringing over the bread basket. After offering the basket's contents to his mother who summarily dismissed him, Efraim turned to Molly. Clicking his heels together and bowing, he produced the challah as if it were a Faberge egg. Molly reached out to break off a piece of bread and was amazed to find herself flustered. *Am I actually blushing?*

"Miss Marina, as you will be staying with us for some time, perhaps you will allow me to escort you to the assemblies on Tuesday next?" Ysroel said, the first one to venture a solicitation. "I hear a famous quartet from Kiev will be performing, and it would be my great pleasure if you would agree to attend."

"That is very kind of you, but..."

"Perhaps, Miss Marina prefers poetry," Efraim jumped into the mix. "Would you do me the honor of accompanying me to the University on Sunday afternoon? I am certain you would enjoy the program."

Benjamin—last, but not least—added his request. "And may I have the honor of escorting you to tea afterwards. I know a charming tea room, the finest in Odessa."

Molly observed Leah watching her brothers with great amusement. She looked like a modern-day tennis fan, going from brother to brother, back and forth. Bobe Malka, on the other hand, was looking straight ahead as if the detail on the draperies required her utmost attention. The only perceivable motion was that of her spoon being dipped ever so gently into her soup.

Unbeknownst to Molly, her hostess was enjoying herself exceedingly. Malka had foreseen this predicament—knowing her sons all too well. What was yet to be witnessed was how her young guest would handle the milieu. After all, had she not implied just moments ago that she could *not* handle impromptu situations?

Strangely, Molly, who usually was one to address a problem from all sides, calculating risks and probable outcomes, did take charge of the matter with little hesitation. "I do apologize, gentlemen, but I cannot accept your kind and generous offers," said she. "I am certain that my intended would not approve of such outings."

Hearing such a declaration, Leah choked on her soup in a most unladylike fashion.

"Your intended?" Malka repeated, surprised, yet pleased with the girl's clever retort.

"Yes, of course, Mama," Leah said, with regained composure. "Her intended—Dr. Zhivago."

It was Molly's turn to cough in a most unbecoming manner, but the awkward situation seemed to be resolved. Her would-be suitors returned to their seats—and to their meal—with much less gusto than originally anticipated. Molly and Leah beamed at each other from across the table. At least one fiasco was averted as the family returned their attention to polite conversation and the next course of chopped liver with onions. Avram, however, was not prepared to discontinue his line of questioning.

"Miss Marina, how is the situation in Lvov these days? How are our people faring?"

Molly allowed herself to smile. *This I can answer*.

"It may well depend on whom you ask, Avram. The wealthy merchants and students of Lvov University are busy promoting the Jewish enlightenment. Those involved in the Haskalah movement, encourage our people to study Russian and to continue with their education. There are many who are leaving the *yeshivot*. They are pursuing nonspiritual studies and attempting to assimilate into the secular world. And, of course, the Zionist movement is continuing to gain momentum."

"Miss Marina," Avram replied, "you are not quite like the young ladies in Odessa, are you? I do not believe my sisters have any notion of these matters."

"You asked me a question and I simply responded. My father enjoys sharing the news of the day," she quickly added. "It is not unusual for us to debate these matters at our dinner table."

"And what of the traditional Jews, or do you only speak of assimilation and enlightenment?"

"Quite the contrary, I assure you. My father enjoys a balanced discussion; therefore, we speak of the Hasidim with great reverence. As you know, Lvov has been at the very center of the Hasidic movement from the onset. But at the other end of the spectrum, the Reform synagogue that was built in 1844 is also growing in popularity."

"Reformation is an interesting concept. It is thanks to the growing Zionist organizations that we have innovative and enlightening periodicals," Yosef eagerly interjected. "The Zionists have formed several youth groups that support our new vision for the future. This is where my interest lies."

"Your interests—ha! You've been reading Levanda and Rabinovich again, haven't you Brother?" Avram reproached.

Molly, who was desperately trying to remain calm and nonchalant, hastily responded. "I, for one, would be very interested in hearing your opinion, Yosef." *I am sitting at the dinner table with my great grandfather—discussing current events. Somebody pinch me!*

"I find that Lev Levanda's writings have much to say about our present situation," said Yosef, glaring at his sibling. "I know that you do not agree with his outspoken critique of Jewish traditionalism, Avram, but he is an advocate for our people. And what's more, I believe that he has shown himself to be rather conservative in his approach. As for Osip Rabinovich, someone who rejects Russian anti-Semitism—"

Sensing the need to change the subject, Malka attempted to turn the conversation. "Marina, my dear, do you like fish?"

"I must admit, I am not an avid fan of the dish. My mother, however, is a wonderful cook and she likes to prepare gefilte fish for special occasions."

"Ah. Our little Gitel also had an aversion to fish, but I think we have been able to change her mind."

"Mama, she is not 'our little Gitel'. She is an under maid," Naftali gently reminded.

"Oh, is that what we are calling her these days?" Avram's wife scoffed.

"Bluma dear, we have yet to make a determination. Gitel has only been with us for a short time due to some rather unfortunate circumstances," Malka said, offering an explanation to Molly. "She may make a fine chamber maid, or she may be better suited to assist in the kitchen. I have not yet made up my mind. In any event," she continued, "along with the potato kugel and mutton, Mrs. Kraskov has prepared salmon for us tonight. I do hope you will enjoy it."

"Yes, well—enough talk about food and household staff. I am quite certain Miss Marina is not interested in these domiciliary issues. As for myself," said Rivka, a bit out of synch, "I enjoy the cultural life here in Odessa. We have a Jewish theater and literature in Hebrew and Yiddish. The city is overflowing with such lively entertainment and educated, interesting people. It is quite lovely. I am certain you will enjoy your visit with us."

"*A sof*, Rivka. Enough of that superficial nonsense. You paint such a picture, Miss Marina will return to Lvov thinking this is a paradise!" Yosef exclaimed. "There has been an increase in anti-Semitism parallel to the success of our people. With every step forward, the non-Jewish community has lashed out in anger and jealousy. The Russians detest the Ukrainians. The Ukrainians despise the Poles, and everyone hates the Jews! Avram, you criticize me for reading Levanda and Rabinovich, but here you have a greater offense—Rivka lives in the dream world of Pushkin and Dostoyevsky!"

"I believe things have been deteriorating all across the empire ever since Tsar Alexander II was assassinated, is it not so?" Molly asked, trying to needle her way back into the conversation. "The last several years have seen pogroms, murder and rape..."

"Marina, my dear—" Malka began to reproach. This sort of inflammatory conversation was exactly what she had been trying to avoid.

"Miss Marina, I am astonished at your observations. Does your father allow you to speak of such things?" The entire room had become silent. Avram's piercing question found its mark.

Silverware and goblets of wine were set down. Everyone had turned to stare at their guest. What kind of young lady spoke in this manner? Laughter from the other end of the table broke the uncomfortable silence.

"Avram, she is a Galitsyaner! What do you expect? Dry, boring conversation?" Once again, Leah had come to Molly's rescue.

"I do not care if she is a Siberian Tatar, Miss Marina is absolutely right. I find it refreshing that a young woman is knowledgeable about the facts," Yosef pronounced. "For decades now, anarchy has reigned over our people. The Jews are blamed for everything, and what is most shocking, is that we are not talking about uneducated Cossacks or village peasants. We are talking about Russian intellectuals—even they are fighting against us! Our people have been prohibited from living where they choose. There have been restrictions placed on how many of us may study in secular schools. The propaganda machine against the Jews is churning out more and more rubbish each day."

"This is not quite the dinner conversation I had in mind for tonight, my dears. Our young guest will not soon wish to return. Let us enjoy our fruit compote and finish our meal in peace."

"It is quite alright, Bobe Malka. I am very aware of the politics of the day. I am not frightened or scandalized."

"*Bobe Malka*?" Avram repeated. "What is the meaning of this?"

"Ah—yes. Forgive my informality," Molly stammered. "It is my Galitsyaner ways, I suppose. I must seem like a country bumpkin amongst esteemed family."

"Not at all, Miss Marina," Benjamin declared, glaring at his brother. "You are very charming indeed."

With dinner now completed, those so inclined, participated in *benching*—the recitation of the Birkat Hamazon prayers. The ladies then proceeded into the drawing room. Molly, at once, was both relieved and irritated. She recalled that her grandfather always commented that the *sobremesa* in Argentina was the best part of a gathering. Although things had become a bit heated, she would have loved to continue with the banter.

"Why should we be relegated to another room," she asked, "while the men enjoy their after-dinner conversation?"

"Miss Marina, you *do* have a Polishe way of looking at things," Bluma replied. "I rather enjoy removing myself from the table and the tiring conversation. Of course, you seemed to be hanging on every word—especially when Yosef was speaking—and I must say; you were blushing when he praised your knowledge of current events."

"Marina," Leah interrupted, "do look at it in a different light. The men must stay cramped and cloistered around a messy dinner table, while we may recline comfortably in this charming room and speak of whatever we desire—without censure."

"I suppose you do have a point. And it is quite charming in here," Molly said, as she took a turn about the room before settling down on a divan. She eyed the evening tea which had been set out. A silver samovar was situated at the center of the table encircled by a grouping of *podstakannik.* The fine, etched crystal glasses were enfolded in delicate work of silver and gold filigree. "This is a beautiful home. I had no idea that you lived like this..." Molly nearly bit her tongue. She already had gotten herself into trouble with her childish comments. She needed to be mindful of her reactions—and that included trying not to blush.

"Yes, we are very fortunate, my dear," Malka paused to offer her guest a tray of chocolates and petit fours. "My husband toiled under the most treacherous circumstances in order to provide for his family...but we have a saying here: 'Treasure is not required when there is harmony in the family.' I would live in a wooden shack, if my children would simply all get along. However, a family is only a small mirror of the outside world. I dare say, our differences reflect what is being experienced in the community at large."

"How did your husband manage such great success in this political atmosphere, and since you mentioned it," Molly couldn't help but ask, "why is Avram so hostile?" Of course, she knew her questions would be perceived as insolent and ill-mannered by the other women in the room, but she was willing to risk their ire.

Astute as always, Malka realized that her great-great-granddaughter's questioning stemmed from the essence of who she truly was—a historian at heart. "I suppose to tell the tale one must go back to the late 1700's—1799 to be exact. Solomon's family, as well as mine, emigrated from Lithuania as treaties had been declared and new opportunities were available to the Jewish peoples. Our families settled in the north western provinces of what is known as the Pale."

Molly, sitting on the edge of her chair, was soaking in the information and wishing desperately to have pen and paper to write it all down. She and her father never knew about the Lithuania connection, although it was always intimated that the family had Prussian ancestry.

"It was during the early half of the nineteenth century that many Jews from these provinces migrated to Novorossiya—the new Russia," Malka continued. "Of course, this was only possibly because permission was granted and *that* was solely motivated by economics. Educated people were needed in these new areas. Skilled people, such as artisans, tailors, educators, and merchants, were much sought after."

"Yes, of course," Molly interrupted, "Because of the destructive impact of the Crimean War on Black Sea trade."

"The Crimean War did much more than destroy trade. The diseases alone..."

"Yes Bluma, dear," Malka gently replied to her daughter-in-law. "Marina, you are correct. Many in the Jewish communities achieved predominance in grain and textiles at this time, as did Solomon's father. Although movement outside of certain areas was prohibitive, Jewish merchants of the First Guild had the right to live outside the Pale of Settlement. By the time Solomon and I were married in 1865, he and his family were quite successful. They had been involved in the manufacturing and exportation of textiles, and were members of the Guild. On occasion, I was fortunate to accompany my husband on business trips to Paris—of course, that was many years ago."

1865! Remember the marriage date of 1865!

"Solomon had been taught by his father and uncles how to best the oppressors and to beat them in their own game," Malka continued. "The family had accumulated a considerable amount of wealth and they invested in industrial development. Thus, the community witnessed the emergence of a Jewish bourgeoisie. This was allowed when the authorities began realizing the beneficial role of a contributing Jewish populace to the Russian economy."

"I am fascinated by this information, Bobe Malka," Molly replied.

"I find that odd. Surely, this information, as you call it, pertains to your own family's success" Bluma charged. "Is not your father an associate of ours? As a Jew, his trajectory in the business world could not have varied by much."

"Be that as it may, I find it fascinating to hear Solomon and Malka's journey, as it differs from my family's version—ever so slightly." Molly wanted her illustrious ancestor to continue and hoped that she wouldn't have to fabricate a different story to satisfy Bluma's biting curiosity. She decided to pick up where Bobe Malka left off. "Of course, when Nicolas II reign began, the situation for all of us deteriorated."

"Quite so. Solomon's obsession with our safety was the impetus for purchasing this home. It was large enough to hold our growing brood, and eventually, their new families. He would not abide independent households or long distances of separation. He believed the family was stronger living under one roof. However, the current situation in our communities is causing a rift between the brothers, you see," Malka paused for a moment. Saddened by her own comment, she sipped her tea as if gathering strength to continue.

"My younger sons are becoming more and more politically inclined. They are looking towards the future and seeking freedom from tyranny. Avram and the others are against modernization and assimilation, because they fear we are losing our traditions and culture. My daughters are caught in the middle. Thankfully, Sara and Rivka are married to wise and good men. Leah is the last of my girls, and it is proving a difficult scenario to make a good match."

The men, boisterously entering the drawing room, interrupted their intimate conversation. The women instinctively adjusted their posture and their train of thought. Suddenly the conversation turned to tea cookies—Russian, of course—and how the samovar was in dire need of polishing. *It was not!*

Molly knew that further discussion about history or politics would have to wait for another day. She only hoped that another opportunity would arise soon. She wasn't counting on being in 1900 for too much longer.

CHAPTER SIX

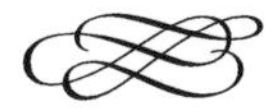

8th of April

Saturday had been a long day of reflection, prayers, and eating. Being unaccustomed to observing a traditional Sabbath with all its rites and regulations, Molly happily accepted the challenge as a sociologist's experiment, more than a religious undertaking.

Upon returning from morning services, a delightful luncheon of fish and *cholent* was served. She was pleasantly surprised with the meal, as neither entrée would have been her first choice under normal circumstances. She made a point of thanking Mrs. Kraskov and even went as far as asking her for the gefilte fish recipe. *Wouldn't Mom be surprised if I made this for Passover*?

"You must use pike, or other freshwater fish," Mrs.

Kraskov replied, pleased to share her secrets. "My mother was *Polishe*, you see, and at home, we used to slice the fish into steaks. Then we'd remove the flesh from the spine and ribs.

Make sure you leave the skin intact, because the next step is to fill the space between the skin and bones with a mixture of chopped fish, breadcrumbs, egg, onions, and a little salt, pepper, and sugar. As you know—since you are from Lvov—sugar is the Polishe part!"

"Thank you, Mrs. Kraskov, but I'm sure there is no need to discuss the recipe in such graphic detail." Having a penchant for interrupting, Bluma had to have her share of the conversation.

Malka inclined her head ever so slightly. The cook took it as a sign of encouragement and continued, disregarding Bluma's intent to dismiss her.

"Next you must poach the steaks in water with onions and carrots, and serve them cold with the jellied stock. Of course, if you do not wish to do a whole fish and make steaks, you can make the balls and wrap them with the skin. That way the balls are considered *gefilt*—stuffed!"

Molly hesitated a moment, just to make sure the woman had had her say. It was a flushed Mrs. Kraskov who stood before the family, arms folded under her ample bosom, waiting to be prompted further.

"It is absolutely delicious," said Molly. "I will be sure to tell my mother. And the cholent? I never had..."

"You have never had cholent?" asked the shocked cook.

"Well, not like this," she fibbed. "May I ask, what is your secret?

"The secret is with the pot. It was my grandmother's. I will show you. It is quite old."

Mrs. Kraskov beamed as she stepped away for a moment only to return with her family heirloom for inspection. Molly was duly impressed. The container was made of hammered copper and had the word *Shabbos* embossed across the center. She estimated the antique was well over one hundred years old.

"How lovely to have such a keepsake."

"We have prepared cholent in this pot for generations. The pot works wonders, but I am also thankful to Mr. Avram for ensuring our kitchen was equipped with a proper oven. You see, I place it in our baker's oven before sunset on Shabbes. The oven remains hot all through Friday and midday Saturday. The food is gently simmered for hours, until it's ready for our Shabbes afternoon meal. Truth be told, it was all Mr. Avram's idea."

Molly was doubly impressed, both by the cook's skill and Avram for his innovation. "Thank you so very much for sharing your secrets, Mrs. Kraskov. I've learned quite a bit today."

Molly caught Bobe Malka's eye. Glowing with pride, the matriarch had approved of the conversation. She was pleased that Molly showed interest in the old cook's stories. But this was what Molly thrived on. It was only natural for her to ask questions about family traditions and history. She had enjoyed the listening as much as Mrs. Kraskov enjoyed the sharing.

The remainder of the day was spent napping, with the occasional stroll about the garden. In Molly's case, it was actually three strolls about the garden. She was jumping out of her skin, not accustomed to so much down time. With her mind racing, and desperately trying to regain some sort of normalcy, she had asked for pen and paper to jot down some notes. Of course, she hadn't realized the impropriety of her request. Writing was not permitted on Shabbes, however, she was not overly disappointed—yesterday's fiasco still being fresh in her mind.

Gitel had been instructed to bring writing supplies to Molly's room before the Sabbath had begun. The household didn't have any of the *newfangled* reservoir pens. They relied on a fickle instrument which Molly couldn't seem to conquer. On her first few attempts and using a conservative amount of ink, she had torn the thin sheet of paper with the dry, metal nib. Thinking she understood her error, she dipped into the inkwell again with a heavier hand, but the end result was something that resembled a Rorschach ink blot test—the kind used in Psychology 101. Thankfully, she had thrown on the pinafore that Gitel provided. With the rough, linen apron stained beyond repair and her fingers freckled with large black spots, she had decided that she was not in the right frame of mind to learn a new skill and was thankful no one was around to witness her ineptness. When she was reminded that writing was not considered *shomer Shabbes*, Molly decided to go back out for another walk in the garden.

The lush green lawn was enveloped by shrubbery, each square divided by a pebbled pathway. The flowers, although they appeared to grow in wild abandon, were carefully tended to by both laborers and family alike. Bobe Malka had mentioned at breakfast that some of the ladies enjoyed pruning the roses and smaller fruit trees. Dvora, Duvid's mother, and Bluma were quite skilled at picking just the right blooms and creating arrangements for the household. This came as a surprise to Molly as she had only witnessed Bluma as Avram's pallid and habitually-cross wife. She couldn't imagine her working in the gardens, and yet, it was there that Molly found her.

Bluma stood alongside a happy patch of sunflowers, but her gaze was elsewhere. Alone in her thoughts, her cheeks were flushed and the color made her appear youthful and rejuvenated. Molly had almost turned away, not wanting to have an awkward exchange, but it was too late. Bluma had acknowledged her presence and Molly felt quite the interloper.

"Please forgive me, Bluma," she murmured. "I didn't mean to interrupt your afternoon walk. You looked quite...peaceful. Happy, to be exact."

"Happy? I? And that surprises you, does it not?"

Molly didn't have a clue how to respond.

"That is quite alright," Bluma replied. "Do not trouble yourself. I know how I appear to you. I know that it is uncomfortable to be in my company. It is uncomfortable for *me* as well."

"I didn't mean to insinuate anything..."

"Come, come, Marina. It is Shabbes, after all. We mustn't lie or tell half-truths."

"I wasn't lying. You looked peaceful. You seemed to be day dreaming."

"Ah, yes. Day dreaming. The flowers remind me of happier days," she said, inhaling the scent of a vibrant bloom. "My parents had six children—all girls. We, each of us, were named to honor the flora of Papa's garden. I was the eldest and he named me Bluma. Sometimes he would simply call me 'beautiful flower.' I would spend hours in the garden—traipsing after him, happy and carefree. Mama would reprimand us both, for I should have been indoors helping with the household chores or watching over my younger sisters. But Papa would have none of it. He said there would be plenty of time for cooking and cleaning and child rearing."

Bluma sank onto the cushions of a wooden bench. Molly waited for her to continue, uncomfortable in the silence.

"There can be nothing of beauty now. All the flowers are gone."

"What do you mean?"

"One by one, my sisters fell ill. It was the Cholera—a lingering consequence of the Crimean War. Mama worked herself to death caring for them. Papa buried them all, and then, there was no one left to bury poor Papa. Except, of course, for the *Chevra Kadisha*. I was married and far away from home. I was expecting our first child..." she stopped and sighed deeply. "But it was not meant to be. We lost the child as well. The physician said it was due to the emotional blow I had suffered."

"I am so sorry..."

"And yet, we tried again. Everyone said it was for the best. Avram hoped that a child would bring back the color in my cheeks," she said in a whisper. "And I conceived another child. And again, it was not meant to be. The child was laying transverse in my womb. We both suffered hours on end, but the physician was not able to turn him. The doctor, who had trained with a German obstetrician, begged Avram to allow him to perform a newly-perfected technique. And while I was screaming for Hashem to take us both, Avram gave his permission for the operation. The child was delivered by Cesarean section, and I had given birth to a son. He was small and didn't cry at once. But weak as he was, he survived. We had to wait a month complete before we could send for the *mohel*. The rabbi had given us permission to postpone the *bris*, because the child needed to gain strength. Finally the mohel came; Moishe was the child's *sandek*. It was he who praised Hashem for the many blessings of the day—that a son had been born to the family—that he had grown strong enough to enter the covenant. The mohel questioned the delay, and upon hearing that the child was not born naturally—that he did not open the womb—I was told that this son did not count as a first born. The rabbi said I should try again next year..."

"Bluma, this can't be true!"

"But it is true! And I was weak and I did not utter a word against these learned men. And my milk was sour because I became so. And my child, who was already weak, did not survive."

"Was Avram...? Was he cruel to you?"

"Oh no. Avram and I were happy in the beginning. He loved me then—he loves me still. He means well, but in fighting his own desperation, he tries to dissipate mine with psalms and proverbs. I'm overwhelmed with lectures and—inadvertently—am made to feel ashamed."

"But why?"

"Because in my grief, he only hears anger—anger towards Hashem. He instructs me to have faith and to pray for understanding and for patience. I just want to be left alone. I want to grieve."

The two women sat together for several minutes; Bluma emotionally spent and Molly in utter and complete dismay. What could she possibly say? Who was she to offer any words of wisdom? Bluma broke the silence instead.

"I beg your pardon. I do not know what has come over me. I do so rarely speak of the matter..."

"Please don't apologize. You are depressed and angry. Look Bluma, I don't know much about these things—I know even less about psalms and proverbs—but I don't think it is wrong to question God. Didn't Jacob wrestle with the angel? Moses himself argued and railed against the Lord. And ..." Molly paused and recalled a recent conversation with her mother. "And then there is

Rachel...one of the Matriarchs! My mother was just talking about Rachel and her tears..."

Molly was up now, pacing back and forth. She must have seemed possessed as she tried to recall the message her mother had tried to share. "Okay, now bear with me because I don't remember the whole thing. Mom was talking about the Tree of Life and Rachel and her maternal love. I'm sure I've got it all mixed up, but there was a point to this. Rachel is—um—was—no—*is* the epitome of dignity..."

Molly's stumbling jolted Bluma out of her passive state. She sharply interrupted the strange girl.

"Really Miss Marina! I truly do not need another lecture, especially from an unmarried, uneducated..."

"Wait, please. I remember the point of the story."

"Why should I listen to you—a foreigner—an outsider? Why, you cannot even put two words together without stuttering and tripping over your own thoughts. Who are you to speak to me thus?"

Molly felt the color come to her cheeks. "I was only trying to help. Just as my mother was trying to help me with something she had read about Rachel, but I was too stubborn to listen. You're right. I am stuttering, but if you would come down off that high horse and just listen to me for a moment, you might get something out of it!"

Bluma was in a state of shock. No one had ever spoken to her in this manner. In fact most of the time, no one spoke to her at all. Out of curiosity, she nodded her head once and gave Molly permission to continue.

"Am I right to think that you feel insecure and unworthy of Avram's love?"

"Well, yes—this is true. Avram deserves a wife that can provide him with healthy children. He deserves a wife that can bring him joy."

"That's just it. You are forgetting your own inherent value —*your value*—as an individual. You, all by yourself, are worthy and that sense of worth is the direct antitheses to shame and self-recrimination. You are depressed because you have been hit hard by life, but maybe, you should think of Rachel's story. Try to evoke some compassion for yourself. I mean—give yourself a break!"

"You do speak strangely; but perhaps because you found me here in this wretched, weakened state, I am more inclined to heed your words. After all, it is the way of our people to carry on..."

"By all means, carry on, but allow yourself some time. Grieving is part of the healing process." Molly stopped short as an image suddenly popped into her mind. It was the image of a woman disembarking a ship holding her newborn son. She remembered her grandfather's story of the relative who gave birth while traveling to Argentina. *Was that Bluma?* She couldn't say for sure and she wouldn't risk saying too much more. "Please Bluma. Just don't give up hope."

The sun was beginning to set. Soon Shabbes would be over. Bluma stood and opened her arms to envelop the tall stalks of cheerful sunflowers—her father's favorite.

"Papa used to say that sunflowers are a reminder of the Source of Life and all that is good." She turned now and faced the stranger from Lvov. "I am grateful to you, Marina. I believe that this unusual *d'var Torah* of yours has helped me immeasurably."

"I am so pleased. Shall we go in? It's getting dark."

"I believe I will remain outdoors for a while longer. *Shavua Tov*, Marina. May you have a good week."

"Shavua Tov," she replied and quickly made for the first door she could find. Molly wanted nothing more than to return to her room and to avoid further confrontations. What was she thinking? She was not equipped to carry on complex—religious—conversations with her twentieth century relatives. She was out of her element, and the sooner she realized that she should keep her mouth shut, the better.

Unfortunately her plan to go unnoticed was foiled; for as she was returning to her room, Molly crossed paths with Bobe Malka on the grand staircase.

"I was just coming to see how you were faring—what is it? What has happened" Seeing the girl visibly shaken, Malka guided her to a nearby settee in the hallway. "My dear, you are shivering."

Molly quickly explained the exchange of words she had with Bluma in the garden. "After everything she has been through, the thing that gets me the most is the callousness of the mohel. Is this how a man of God should speak? Where is his compassion?"

Malka had been careful not to interrupt while Molly shared her story. She wanted to measure her words, uncertain if the girl would grasp her meaning. Not that she wasn't intelligent; but after all, they had only just met. She needed to consider the emotional state of her guest, as well as her grasp of *frum* culture and tradition. She didn't wish to excuse the mohel. His words were insensitive, but perhaps she could explain that his purpose was well-intentioned.

"My dear, it is sadly true that these words were spoken to poor Bluma. But consider for a moment the source. The mohel's vocation is to perform the bris—it is a *mitzvah*—a joyful and emotive commandment we observe in our attempt to live a holy life. His objective is to see each one reach this higher plane, but quite possibly, in his obsession to work towards his goal, he only sees the end result. Perhaps this is the secret of our People. In the darkest of times, it is our faith that moves us onward—always forward. Each morning, when we rise, we say the *Modah Ani*, thanking Hashem for a new day, for a new chance to do better—to be better. Perhaps the mohel only meant to inspire Bluma."

Gripping her hands, Molly simply shook her head. "Where do you find the strength to go on when you have been beaten down so cruelly? I can't fathom..."

"My dear, you do not go on for yourself alone. You find the strength for those around you, and for those yet to come who depend upon you to survive and thrive. You spoke well to Bluma. I am pleased with what you have told me."

"But they weren't my words. They were my mother's. She had been trying to build up my confidence, and of course, Mom reverted to her new-age vernacular. I had been only half listening, but under the circumstances, the words seemed fitting for Bluma. But that doesn't excuse the mohel! What if it was his fault that she wasn't able to nurse the baby? What if he had offered a kind word of encouragement, instead of discounting Bluma's newborn son?"

"What are you implying, malyshka? That the mohel's comments allowed for the Evil Eye to harm the child?"

"What? No! I'm saying that someone like that should know better. You don't tell a woman that this baby doesn't count or try again next year. My head is reeling at his insensitivity. Poor Bluma! Poor Avram.

"Yes, those two wretched souls have been through quite enough. May the good Lord bless them only with *naches* from this time forward," Malka stood and stretched out her hand. "Now then, go fetch a shawl and join us downstairs in the parlor—but my dear, do try limiting your speech to current events. Mentioning your mother is an invitation for further questioning."

As the evening came to close, Molly reviewed the day's events and her reactions. Under these extraordinary circumstances, she did well. She surprised herself, actually, and wondered what Michael would think if he could see her now...flying by the seat of her pants.

Full of energy and enthusiastic for what was to come, she was anxious for the new week to begin. Bobe Malka had promised that they would go into town and begin their search for the fabled tarot card.

If all else fails, I will click my heels together and repeat: There's no place like home, there's no place like home.

CHAPTER SEVEN

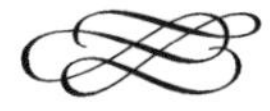

9th of April

Bright and early Sunday morning, Molly eagerly began preparing for the new day. She had been made fully aware—nearly from the beginning of this adventure—that the third floor had not been modernized as of yet. For all the elegance and opulence of the home, the bathroom accommodations were still quite Victorian. She washed her face in ice-cold water she had poured from the pitcher into a porcelain bowl. She desperately missed her electric toothbrush and the heated bathroom floor at home.

Gitel came to her room, and begging her pardon, offered a cup of *bavarke*—just a little something to warm and comfort the miss before breakfast. The hot water mixed with milk certainly was an acquired taste, but Molly took a few tentative sips as she contemplated the dressing screen. She groaned at the sight of the corset. Her own bra, T-shirt, and jeans were hidden in a satchel under the bed. The dress she wore yesterday was in the armoire, along with an evening gown. The obvious choice was the burgundy and gold wool dress that Leah was kind enough to loan. Molly had to admit that the gown was lovely. The gigot sleeves had large flowers embroidered with gold thread. The same applique was sparingly used on the form fitting bodice and around the edges of the flared skirt.

As she began the process of slipping on the undergarments, Bobe Malka knocked and entered the room bearing yet another gown.

Molly chuckled at the sight. "Leah must have quite an extensive wardrobe."

"It is a luxury we women allow ourselves in this household, my dear. All my girls have beautiful gowns. We have a saying here: You cannot forbid living beautifully."

Molly was about to say that her travel guide, Galina Alexsandrovich, was also prone to spouting local proverbs, but she held her tongue—chastising herself once more for apparently being unable to keep her promise. Instead, she returned her focus onto the new gown. Wearing this magnificent outfit, she thought, would be a history lesson brought to life. The ensemble was the epitome of Victorian sophistication. Fashioned from a pink floral silk, the dress was embellished with velvet trim and ivory silk chiffon. Molly couldn't help but giggle as she toyed with flounces of beige lace stitched prettily on the dainty sleeves.

"There's something quite ironic about all this. I disliked playing dress up, when I was a little girl. My mother loved costumes—you know, fairies, princesses, and such, but it never suited me. Mom wanted to open up my creative side, you see. She loved stories of nobility, —damsels and knights, queens and their courts. I played along, but it really wasn't my thing. I didn't feel royal, and that whole damsel-in-distress story line was definitely not for me."

"You are speaking of your mother, my dear. I should not hear these things. Please..."

"Oh yes—I'm sorry. I can't tell you how difficult it is to keep track of what I'm saying. It is harder than I would have imagined. And I just stopped myself a moment ago—"

"As for the damsels in distress, I have found in literature, as well as in life, it is not the damsel who needs the rescuing as much as the knight who needs an excuse for action," Malka explained. "In Judaism the sages say, 'The poor man does more for the giver than the giver does for the poor man.' Why do you suppose that is?"

"I'm sorry," said Molly. "I don't know what you mean."

"The poor man gives the *tzaddik* the opportunity to perform a mitzvah. Seen in this light, my dear, maybe your damsel is wiser than you give her credit."

Molly felt herself blush, but rather than capitulate—she and her father were used to going several rounds before someone would cry uncle—she continued with her debate. Qualifying the previous comment, Molly continued with her original complaint.

"If the damsel was so wise, how come she allowed herself to be caged in to these corset contraptions? They're stifling! Why do we need to dress like this, while the men walk about and breathe freely? Why are women treated like dolls, having to look pretty but only speak of petty, insignificant things? I am used to studying and completing research. This *damsel* spends endless hours with her nose stuck in a book. It doesn't matter what I wear or if my hair is properly coiffed."

"Malyshka, you surprise me. How is it possible that you are so highly educated, yet feel so repressed? Do you feel this way here, among us, or is this a struggle you deal with in your time? Oh dear! Let me rephrase that. Do you know what it is to be an *Eishet Chayil*?"

"Isn't that a prayer recited on Shabbes for the woman of the house?"

"Well yes, but there is a bit more to it, my dear. My father, as I told you, spoke highly of the Jewish woman. He would remind us, 'If not for her, the Jewish people would still be enslaved in Egypt.' Think of Miriam and her role. My father would remind us that Moses first offered the Torah to the women when he came down the mountain. It was Jewish women who, time and time again, saved their people through insightfulness, virtue, and belief in God. Think of our mothers, Sara, Rebekah, Leah, and Rachel and those who came after. If not for the Jewish woman, where would we be?"

"I'm not sure how to reply. I haven't researched the subject—"

"There would be no home, Malyshka, no family... no Jewish people. On Friday night, she sits as the queen of her table, while all those around her sing her praises. She is recognized as a Woman of Valor, and rightly so. We, each of us, have our role to play. I can assure you: the corset is not holding my tongue or restraining my thoughts."

Molly examined herself in the mirror. The image surely reflected a different sort of person, but it was not only the physical aspect that had been modified. She prided herself in being a modern woman. Wasn't she educated and open minded? Was it fair to put a generation of Victorian women under a twenty-first century microscope—judging their actions, their goals, and accomplishments?

In just two days' time, she had begun witnessing an interesting transformation in her reactions and thought processes. *Maybe this was what Mom was trying to get me to understand all along.*

"Come now," Malka suddenly exclaimed. "You've spent sufficient time woolgathering, my dear. Our expedition awaits. Let us hope that we are successful in our mission to find the Queen of Eight Wands."

The two women found Leah and Duvid waiting patiently in the foyer—Leah clad in a stunning day-dress of emerald green velvet with an accompanying soutache jacket and Duvid in a black and white checkered wool suit.

"We are ready, Matushka," said Leah, gently adjusting her gloves.

"I wasn't aware that an invitation had been extended, Daughter, but very well. You both appear eager, and you certainly took the time with your *toilette*. I will not be ashamed to be seen about town with you in tow."

Leah and Duvid shared a laugh, knowing that it was all said in jest. Leah hooked her arm through Molly's. Duvid gave his arm to his grandmother and off they went. Within a few blocks, they had left the residential area and Molly found herself walking in the city center.

I was just here, driving down these cobblestone streets with that crazy taxi driver.

The original planners had done a remarkable job of shaping the city. The streets, lined with acacia trees, were laid out beautifully; and around town, a splendid prospect of the shoreline was often in full view. Playing tour guide, Duvid informed Molly that if they were to cross two streets and walk less than a mile to the left, they'd find themselves at the edge of the promontory overlooking the Black Sea. He suggested that they take advantage of the opportunity to view the site.

"Perhaps another day, Duvid. Our business requires that we stay in town this morning," replied Malka.

They resumed their stroll and Molly continued her appreciation of the surroundings. She voiced her fascination with the architecture—each building a classic representation of another style.

"Where is the Grand Theater?" she asked. "I would love to see it. It was built in 1887, I believe, and was considered one of the world's finest. And the opera house! I think it was built in 1810. Oh no—we can skip that one. It was destroyed, wasn't it, in a fire..."

"Marina..."

"Darn it!" She had the decency to blush. "I'm a lost cause."

"Never mind that now," said Malka. "We have arrived. This establishment might have what we are seeking; but please, my dear, let me do the enquiring."

The charming bookshop was well equipped with shelves filled with ancient tomes, secular histories, and novels both in Russian and Yiddish. The building itself was a simple wooden structure, but the polished floors, checkered window treatments, and thick rugs made the space warm and inviting. Slightly off in a corner was a dedicated area for ritual objects found in a Jewish home: *mezuzot, kiddush* cups, Shabbes candlesticks, *Havdalah* sets, and more.

Mordachai, the proprietor, came rushing out from the backroom to greet his clientele. Malka Abramovitz was a well-known and respected customer and he didn't like to keep this caliber of patron waiting.

Seeing Bobe Malka attended, Molly began to peruse the Judaica section and came across a multitude of playing cards. She was instantly reminded of her grandparents playing *naipes* in Argentina. One deck in particular caught her eye as the images were not the usual characters. These were biblical figures: King Solomon, the Queen of Sheba, King David, and Queen Bathsheba. Hebrew lettering was artistically imprinted in a rich shade of cobalt blue. She eagerly looked through the deck, but soon realized that these were not tarot cards. They wouldn't be of any use in getting her home.

She turned to locate her companions and found Bobe Malka standing unceremoniously close to the proprietor—vehemently shaking her head side to side.

"Mordachai, I tell you these cards will not do. I am looking for the Queen of Eight Wands."

"Madame Abramovitz, with all due respect," said the befuddled merchant, "You are speaking of *babe maises*! The Queen of Wands...yes. The Eight of Wands...yes! But, the Queen of Eight Wands, no madame—no!"

"Do not pretend to lecture me on *baba maises*, Mordachai. I know your mother's people. I know from where you hail. And I know that you *know*." As much as respectability allowed, Malka leaned in to emphasize her meaning.

Molly strained to listen, but fell short due to the distance that separated the pair. She could only witness the conversation from afar, and when Mordachai escorted Bobe Malka to his back room, she lost all visibility and was left with only the muffled rumblings of their conversation.

"Madame, I have not *seen* this card, but—yes, you are correct. I know of its existence. My great great-grandmother, may she rest in peace, was a great healer from the old country. Her knowledge was legendary in our family and her formulas and methodologies were passed from generation to generation. The apothecary down the street—my cousin Mendel—he learned everything he knows from family traditions."

"That is all very well and good, Mordachai, but what about the tarot?"

"Yes, madame. I am getting to that. Mendel learned about potions and herbs and I learned about—let us just say—I learned about the written word and the oral traditions. I was taught about the Queen of Eight Wands, but I have never seen her. I would not deem it wise to have that particular card in stock. It would not be proper to have it lying about for just any *uneducated* customer. Beware, madame, the misuse of knowledge is a dangerous undertaking."

Frustrated, Malka nodded her head, acknowledging his warning as she abruptly returned to the main salon. She motioned silently for her family to regroup; but no sooner than they stepped foot outside, Molly resumed her relentless questioning.

"This isn't going to work, is it? How do you know that I can return home? Maybe this was just a fluke. Maybe I'm stuck here."

"Fluke?" Duvid giggled. "That is not a word."

"*Sha*, Duvid. The adults are speaking now," his grandmother reprimanded. "Marina, I only know that these things exist. I cannot explain the tarot, as I cannot explain the parting of the Red Sea. It is the same philosophy with regards to the instruction of certain text, such as the Kabbalah. When a child of thirteen is exposed to certain concepts, or sees things which he doesn't understand, it is viewed as magic. It cannot be explained in terms of the laws of physics, or laws of Man, so they are labeled as miracles. Imagine if Duvid were transplanted to your time, my dear. What do you suppose he would make of your world? He would not be able to put things in perspective. Everything would be magical or of the spirit world."

"This brings up another point," Molly challenged. "Why didn't Duvid change places with me? We were both holding the card."

Duvid was listening intently now. He was curious as well, but he didn't dare speak up. His grandmother already had asked him not to interfere.

"The Queen is a symbol as are the wands, my dear," Malka sighed. "The experience was meant for you. At least, this is my interpretation of the events. After all, you carry the name of Malka, the queen of the Tree of Life; and I believe, it was your powerful intention that instigated the magic."

"What are you implying?"

"What was on your mind before you came to us? Were you contemplating a change? Were you at a cross roads? It is very likely, the answers you seek are readily available, my dear, within your own thoughts."

I'll keep my thoughts to myself, thank you very much.

Molly was frightened by the idea that her great- great-grandmother's words were beginning to make some sense. She was at a cross roads. She had been contemplating a change. *Should I tell her about Michael?* Molly decided to continue walking in silence. She was thankful that Malka didn't press her to speak.

They had walked several blocks, passing vendors of various

sorts—the tailor, the cobbler, and even the haberdasher, when Leah began to complain.

"Mama, might we hire a carriage as we continue our search? It would be considerably more expedient, do you not agree?"

"I do not. Next, you will be asking to hire a *troika*."

"Matushka, you exaggerate!" Leah giggled.

"Not at all. Imagine how much faster we could travel behind a team of three horses and led by a maniac driver?" Malka laughed at her own remark. "No, my sweet, speed is not required. Patience and a good eye is what the occasion necessitates. Let us take our time and keep our focus on this next group of merchants."

They came upon an outdoor market where they found farmers and dairymen alongside a variety of craftsmen. Self-conscious and uncomfortable, Molly felt a bit overdressed as they milled about in their finery. She found herself surrounded by the typical peasants of her childhood story books. Women dressed in folk costumes, colorful babushkas and aprons. The men dressed in woolen top coats, boots that reached their knees and *Tevye* caps.

A vendor was briskly at work block printing a peasant skirt. The traditional Slavic artistry of *Vibijka* was well known to Molly and she was enchanted as she watched the woman complete her project. She knew her mother would appreciate the artisan workmanship and was tempted to make a purchase when her delight came to an abrupt stop. *I can't buy a souvenir for my mother! I don't even know how I am getting back and I'm thinking about buying keepsakes. What an idiot!*

Malka spoke to several vendors, but no one seemed to have what they were seeking. An old farmer, standing by his wagon of potatoes and sugar beets, suggested they visit the gypsy camp outside of town. Malka kept this information to herself, only disclosing to her entourage that she had not been successful.

"I am sorry, my dears. The card we seek is not to be found in today's bazaar. But do not despair. I have not given up hope yet."

"This is pointless!" Molly cried out in exasperation. "We're never going to find the exact card."

"We will find the Queen of Eight Wands," Malka said, as she started towards home. We *must*."

"Why does it always be about a queen? I've been chased by this queen all my life. My mother used to place a crown on my head—a cheap, costume crown she picked up in a Halloween store. She'd tell me to 'imagine the possibilities,' to create stories about powerful, intelligent ladies of the realm. My father used to tell me stories of other sorts of women. Women named *Malka*," Molly said, emphasizing the name while ogling her great-great-grandmother. "These women had to be courageous in the face of real danger. Women who had to clothe and feed their children in a new country, where they had no money, no connections, no language—"

"Marina, my dear heart, you are here for a reason. You must take heed of the lessons you are learning. Return to your own time, and take ownership of the name with which you have been blessed."

"I am a not cut out to be a Malka. I am not a leader! I'm not daring or spontaneous. I am a modern-day bluestocking. Michael—um, a friend of mine—wants us to go out and engage the world...to teach and to experience different cultures. I would be content to live with my nose stuck in a book, quietly researching and documenting facts. I am nothing like the women in my father's stories."

Stopping unexpectedly, Malka turned to look at her young charge. She sighed at the torment she found in the girl's eyes.

"Malyshka, in our tradition, when a child is named in honor of a departed relative, that child does not only inherit the qualities of that particular cherished loved one. The tradition says that the inheritance stems from the first one who owned that name. That is not me. It is Malka, the queen in the Tree of Life. Her energy lives within you, her power resonates *within* you. Be yourself. Do not put your ancestors on pedestals. They—we are human beings with faults and weaknesses like everyone else. Do not hide away your abilities. Do not be afraid to experience life."

"But I am afraid! I am afraid that I cannot live up to the name."

Malka embraced the girl and whispered, "We have a saying here: 'Only she who does nothing, makes no mistakes.' Now, let us make haste. I am in dire need of some tea, and maybe a little bit of Mrs. Kraskov's kamishbroit."

"May we stop for just a moment?" Duvid chimed in. "I noticed some of the village children purchasing seeds from the farmer over there—the one with a cart full of pumpkins. May I have a treat for the walk home?"

"Very well, but do not dilly-dally. We must return quickly in time for tea, and afterwards, we must dress for dinner."

The weary group began the journey back home, each quiet within their own thoughts. Duvid was happily munching on his pumpkin seeds. Leah, as usual, was grumbling to herself about ruined stockings. Molly was frustrated at the thought of having to dress—again. At least, she supposed, they would have time for a nap. *I never took naps at home!*

Later that afternoon, once the tea service had concluded, the family retired to their rooms. It was during this time, when the house was still and the only thing that could be heard were the quiet rumblings coming from the kitchen, Leah came to Molly's door with yet another dress.

She was just about to ask why they brought them in one at a time, when Leah, quite decidedly, sat on the edge of the bed and declared that she had an announcement.

"I am desperate and find that I need a confidant. It is as if you were sent by the angels, Marina. I finally can speak with someone who will not judge me—someone who will understand."

"For heaven's sake. You don't have to be so melodramatic. I wasn't sent by angels." *Then again, I don't know who, or what, sent me.*

"Well? Out with it," Molly grumbled.

"I am secretly meeting a gentleman—a lieutenant. He recently arrived from Moscow. His company is stationed here while training new recruits," Leah said excitedly. "We met at an assembly several weeks ago. It was all quite innocent, you see. There was a poetry reading at the University."

"What? You went alone to the University?"

"No, of course not. I was escorted by Benjamin and Efraim. Yosef was already there. He was one of the organizers."

"Alright. So you met a gentleman at the assembly. Isn't that what normally happens at these things? Weren't you properly introduced by someone... matronly?"

"No—no! That is not what happened at all. We met quite by accident. I was just sitting down for tea. I had a cup and saucer in one hand and a plate of cookies in the other. He did not see that I was about to sit in the same chair that he had designated as his own. We—well, we bumped into each other and both promptly landed on our behinds. The chair toppled over, the tea spilled, and the cookies were splattered all over the floor. He was so very gallant, Marina. He immediately got to his feet and helped me up. He removed his handkerchief from his coat pocket and asked permission to wipe the tea and crumbs off the hem of my skirt... why are you laughing?"

"Leah, that is a great way to meet a guy! I might have to remember that for myself."

"Well! Really! Here I am sharing a confidence and this is how you react?"

"Okay. Okay! I'm sorry. Go on with your story. What is the problem? Why the secret?"

"Marina, do try to listen... he is a lieutenant," Leah repeated, determined to make her new friend understand.

"Yes, I got that. So what? Does he need to be a major or a colonel in order to be acceptable?"

"No!"

"Then what?"

"Jewish! He needs to be Jewish! Marina, he is a *lieutenant* in the Russian army."

"You know," Molly paused, desperately trying not to smile, "This is very interesting."

"What is?" Leah asked, incensed beyond measure.

"It's not true what people say about the 'old days' and children doing what they are told. Apparently, nobody does as they are told. Duvid sneaks upstairs to read Kabbalah, and who knows what else. You are sneaking about with a lieutenant... wait a minute. What did you say just now? You have been *meeting* a gentleman? How many times have you seen this guy, and what, exactly, have you been doing, young lady?"

"Marina," said Leah, making a great production of straightening the lace about her embroidered collar, "I would remind you that I am your great-grandaunt—"

"Don't even pretend to throw that in my face. I demand that you tell me the truth. Now!"

"Oh, very well. We have met by appointment twice, and once quite by chance since the assembly—but, it has all been quite proper. We agreed to meet at Sergey's emporium—I did not wish to arrange a meeting at Mordachai's bookshop, you understand. Next, I happened upon him in the tearoom. Yosef and I were out running errands, when he suddenly recalled a previous appointment. He quite abandoned me! To my delight, while I was left waiting for my brother, I enjoyed afternoon tea with my gentleman friend. He took his leave shortly before Yosef's return. Then a few days ago, we met again when I dropped off Duvid's shoes at the cobbler's establishment for repair. You see, I have done nothing improper."

"So, what is the problem?"

"I admire him, and I believe he cares for me. And—he has asked me to meet him at a public ball on Thursday."

"A dance? But you are not allowed to dance with men! What are you thinking? Do you even know how to dance? What did you tell him?"

"I have never been strictly forbidden. There are many in our community who have been to Paris and London. Many girls my age know how to waltz and...my friends have instructed me," Leah said, as she flittered about the room. "I told him that I would attend if I could find someone to accompany me," she said, stopping in front of Molly and grabbing hold of her hands. "He cannot come to call for me. He asked me, but he *cannot* come to the house! Marina, will you accompany me?"

"Absolutely not! There is no way that I am getting involved in this. No way." Suddenly, the significance of what Leah was proposing, hit home. This was no laughing matter. The political climate—aside from the religious objection—was quite enough reason to reject Leah's appeal.

"I believed you to be the one person who would understand. Do you not have a special gentleman friend? Are you not acquainted with the exquisite emotion?"

"Leah, I do understand your feelings. I have been dating a special someone for five years now..."

The young girl gasped and dropped down on the side of the bed. "What is dating?" Leah said, cupping her blushing face. "And what *exactly* have you been doing for five years?"

"Don't be foolish, Leah. Dating means that we...have an understanding. And five years is not so very long considering our age. As a matter of fact, Michael has asked me to marry him, but ..."

Leah shrieked at this declaration. "You have had an offer of marriage? And have you accepted? How can you not understand how *desperately* I wish to attend the ball with my gentleman friend?"

"I have not accepted Michael. I asked him to wait for my answer. We are too young—as are you." Molly affirmed. "You're not ready to enter into a relationship with a gentleman friend, much less with one whom you cannot introduce to your family! I won't accompany you. I won't risk Bobe Malka's disappointment."

Leah burst into tears, and once again, threw herself on the bed. Molly, completely unprepared for the hysterics, walked away and circled the room in frustration. *Go ahead and cry, for all the good it will do you! This is utter nonsense.*

As the minutes wore on, Leah kept up a steady stream of tears and hiccups. Catching her breath, she uttered, "If you will not accompany me, I will attend the ball on my own!"

Molly had been adamant about not falling for the temper tantrum, but hearing this revelation caused her to rethink her decision. She couldn't very well allow the girl to go out by herself, could she?

"Okay, enough! I will go with you, but you have to promise me that you will not do anything foolish with this guy. You won't let him...you won't allow him to take liberties with your person. Is that understood?" Molly began to feel her power. She decided she was going to lay down as many rules and regulations as possible.

"After the dance, there will be no more sneaking around. You will make a decision and you will stand up for yourself. If this is the guy for you, then you better come clean and tell your mother. Better yet, tell Yosef first. Um—maybe have Yosef, Benjamin, and Efraim with you when you tell your mother."

"Oh Marina, thank you! Thank you! I knew you would come to my aid. You will need a ball gown. I have one for myself that will have to do on short notice, but I do not have another for you. I will have to sneak into Rivka's room. Do not concern yourself. She won't miss it. I know exactly which gown will suit. She will not wear it again because it is white, and now that she is married, she may wear whichever color she desires."

"Can't I just wear the pink evening gown I wore for Shabbes?"

"Oh no! Do not be unreasonable. That gown would never do! This is going to be the best evening of my life. We will be the most beautiful women in attendance!"

"We better not get into trouble, Leah. We will need a plan. How will we leave the house unnoticed? How will we get to the ball? I want to know all these details—and soon."

"Yes! Yes! I will arrange everything and you will have final approval," Leah pledged.

The following days brought frenzied jaunts into town rummaging through bookstores, museums, and apothecaries. Bobe Malka even ventured into the gypsy camp hoping to find the infamous tarot. All was done in vain. The missing piece of the puzzle was nowhere to be found.

Tensions were taut and Molly began having second thoughts of escorting Leah to the dance. After everything that Bobe Malka had done, was it right for her to go behind her back? She rationalized that she was doing a mitzvah—she was protecting Leah, for she knew that the girl would go off by herself and that would be a scandal beyond repair.

Maybe I will get points for making a spur of the moment decision. As the saying goes, 'One who does nothing, makes no mistakes!'

CHAPTER EIGHT

13th of April

Thursday morning, Leah discreetly entered her sister's room and, with the expertise of a seasoned cat thief, escaped with the massive ball gown without anyone's notice. That was quite a feat as the household was filled to capacity. One could hardly slip out into the hallway without running into a staff person or a family member. In reality, she *did* run into someone—Gitel, the young servant. The girls were of a similar age but were worlds apart due to social circumstances. Gitel knew not to ask questions, and Leah knew she needn't provide explanations.

Exchanging polite smiles, Gitel executed a quick curtsey as Leah swiftly crossed from the east wing to the west. Reaching the grand staircase, she ran up to the third floor to Molly's chamber. Now breathless, but bursting with enthusiasm, Leah knocked on the door and entered quickly. She anxiously held the gown up for Molly's inspection and waited for a yeah or nay. However, the startling appearance of the teenager and the magnificence of the item she held in her hands left Molly dumbfounded for a moment. She finally realized that the girl was waiting for some sort of response. She gingerly reached out to take hold of the dress.

"This is for me?"

"It is two seasons old; nevertheless, it is still quite acceptable to wear—maybe not in Moscow, but certainly here in Odessa. Do you approve?"

"It is exquisite."

"Yes. Rivka has a good eye for style and fabric. Mama has taught us well, and now you will reap the rewards! Everything is well in hand, Marina. Our plan for this evening will go smoothly, I assure you. I will begin my toilette upon finishing our afternoon tea. Afterwards, I will return to your room and assist you with your preparations."

Molly simply nodded at these proposals and returned her attention to the white satin gown covered with tulle and chiffon. It was expertly embellished with flowers fashioned in silver sequins. A brocade belt fitted in a flattering V shape followed the line of the bodice. Leah had also provided matching shoes of satin with white and silver beading. *This is my mother's dream come true. I'm in a real-live fairytale. Just call me Cinderella.*

Shortly after tea, Leah returned to Molly's room—right on schedule—looking quite stunning in her own gown of cream chiffon. An emerald green paisley applique of lace and beading covered the skirt. Because it was cut from a modern fashion plate, it had a slimmer silhouette than Molly's gown. The satin sash was at the natural waist. A beaded flower placed at her shoulder accented the appealing sweetheart neckline.

Leah had been right to choose the emerald green accent,

Molly thought. It matched the color of her eyes perfectly. When both were finally dressed and quite ready, they stood before the floor length mirror and admired their accomplishments.

"We are breathtaking, are we not, Marina?"

"Yes," she laughed. "I'll admit it. As my mom would say: we look drop-dead gorgeous!"

"As you say, of course," Leah replied, uncertain of the strange maxims her visitor spouted. "Now comes the difficult part. We must leave the house undetected. As we discussed—ad nauseam I must say—we shall leave by way of the old servant's wing. No one lives in that part of the house anymore, and we will have free access to the stairwell which leads out to the vegetable garden."

"How will we get to the ball?"

"I have arranged for transportation to meet us, but not at that back gate. We will have to walk a short distance. Let us pray that we do not ruin our slippers."

"Okay. Sounds like a plan to me. Let's go."

The pair reached the forsaken servant's stairwell with no delay or intervention. They crossed an empty, cold hallway and slipped through to the garden unnoticed. Molly was full of regret and cursed herself every step along the way. *We are going to get caught. I'm an idiot and we are going to get caught!*

Now outside the gate, and powered by sheer adrenaline, they ran down the deserted street, turned a corner, and continued until finding the awaiting conveyance. *And here is my magical pumpkin turned into a coach and four.*

Molly laughed at the image of the fairy-tale carriage, but was actually relieved that it was not a troika as Leah previously insinuated. The fashionable phaeton looked quite comfortable with its high seats and closed back. More importantly, she noted it had a folding roof. Although appreciative of the protection from the cool evening breeze, Molly was more concerned with their traveling about town. The enclosed carriage would help shield them from nosey neighbors.

The footman assisted his passengers aboard. Molly awkwardly stepped into the carriage and nearly tore her gown. Leah, naturally, had an easier time of it. She made a point of gracefully situating herself, and then let out a burst of laughter as the footman closed the door.

"Marina! Whatever is the matter with you?"

"It's this gown and these slippers! There is too much material —I'm not used to all of this finery. I tripped on the first little step and nearly lost my balance."

"Had I boarded the carriage in such a manner, Mama would have lectured me for days," Leah reproved.

"Well, it's a good thing that *Mama* is not here, isn't it— considering where we are going and all."

"Point well taken. Do forgive me."

"Exactly where are we going?" Molly asked, still attempting to situate herself comfortably without creasing the gown. "With all the worrying about getting out of the house, I seem to have forgotten to ask..." *That's a first! Maybe it's some sort of time warp side effect!*

"Did I not tell you? It is terribly exciting! The ball is being held at the Hotel Bristol. The grand opening was just last year, but, of course, we didn't attend. That is to say, I was too young and Mama did not wish to attend. Word about town is that it's magnificent!"

"The Bristol? By the Philharmonic Theater? You know, it's

funny—I tried to book a room there last week, but there was no vacancy."

"Indeed? Oh Marina, do stop talking about architecture and tourist attractions. Have compassion for my nerves! I am all aflutter with anticipation."

"Alright. Calm down," said Molly, sounding a bit schoolmarmish, although she could hardly keep from smiling.

Trying to ignore the jittery teenager, Molly peered out the window attempting to get her bearings. She was grateful that the horses were moving along at a steady, even pace. The streets were dark and her vision was impaired, but she was finally able to decipher a street plaque. They were in the city center on Pushkinska Street—the very street that she had on her 'must-see' list.

The Hotel Bristol was a historical legacy and was located in one of the most popular tourist areas. Situated by the Odessa National Research Library, it had been Molly's first choice for accommodations; however, they were booked solid for the next three months. She had been so very disappointed; but now looking through the carriage window, she couldn't help but laugh at the curious turn of events.

The hotel was ablaze with light. Both candle and gas fixtures illuminated the entrance of the neoclassical work of art. The driver, mindful of the ladies delicate apparel, was careful to bring the horses to a full stop at a most suitable location. With the footman's assistance, Molly and Leah were able to disembark quite easily—without soiling their satin slippers. The driver was given instructions regarding their departure. Molly, yet again, felt a bit like Cinderella, for by the stroke of midnight, they needed to be home, safe and sound.

The women linked arms and together they glided past the Baroque statues guarding the entrance. Leah had no idea, of course, but Molly was well aware that the hotel would close after the Revolution in 1917. It would not reopen until 1928, and in keeping with Soviet Union leadership, it would be renamed Hotel *Krasnaya* (Red). The grand hotel would close once again in 2002 and undergo yet another restoration. That final transformation would allow the well-known establishment to reopen in 2010, under the original name. Taking note of her surroundings, Molly promised herself a return visit in *her* time. What a treat it would be to see the *before* and *after* edition.

They followed the delightful sounds of the orchestra coming from a distant room. Ladies and gentlemen, dressed in their finery, led the way down a handsome promenade. With every other step, Molly insisted on stopping and inspecting the lavish décor. Stunning floral arrangements were placed in Empire-period bronze vases, alternating with candelabras of ormolu and malachite. Multifaceted pendants of cut-glass swayed prettily from the chandeliers, dancing in the shimmering candlelight. Molly was so enthralled by her resplendent surroundings she didn't realize that Leah had walked on ahead. *That little stinker! She's trying to get rid of me.*

Turning her attention now to the ballroom, Molly quickened her pace to catch up with her great-grandaunt. As she walked through the double doors, her suspicions were proven correct. Leah was already dangling on the arm of her lieutenant. It was precisely at that moment that Molly came face to face with Yosef Abramovitz! Shocked, she waited for a stern reproach, hoping that he wouldn't cause a scene.

"Miss Marina!" he cried out. "Whatever are you doing here?"

Think Molly! Think!

"I could ask the same of you, Yosef," she said, proud that she came up with a line, albeit not a very inspired one.

"Is that so? And yet, I am not a young woman attending a public ball—unescorted—and in peril of causing a great scandal."

"Cause a great scandal? I? Don't be ridiculous."

"I do not have time to discuss this matter at length with you, Miss Marina. Suffice it to say, you should not be in attendance, and I question your judgment—*your motives*—in coming here without, I am certain, consulting Mama."

"For heaven's sake," Molly said, poking her delicate fan sharply into his shoulder. "If you must know, I am here to protect your sister!"

"Leah? Here?" said Yosef, as he quickly attempted to conceal himself behind a large potted fern. "She must not see me!"

Molly let out an unladylike snort. "This family would put the Kardashians to shame. So much drama! So much intrigue!"

"I am not acquainted with that family, Miss Marina, but let me assure you, I do not revel in secrecy and schemes. And now, you will pardon me, but I have spied the person I have come to meet," Yosef said, peering from behind his hiding place. "Do make yourself useful, Miss Marina, and guard my sister. As a matter of fact, I beseech you to remove her from the premises at once. But—ah, please do not mention our little tête-á-tête."

Molly sighed and resigned herself to, once more, be a family member's confidant. "I won't tell anyone that I saw you, if you won't tell anyone you saw me."

With a quick bow and a curt, "Good evening," Yosef disappeared.

Molly set out to find her great-grand aunt. Luckily for her,

Leah wasn't hard to find. She simply followed the sound of the schoolgirl's giggles. She approached the couple from the side and was able to get a good look at Leah's dashing officer. Molly had to admit, the man was definitely Prince Charming material. Tall, handsome, and broad shoulders...*He's another character from my mom's books. Mr. Darcy? No—this guy is in uniform—maybe a Colonel Brandon? Good God! I hope he doesn't turn out to be a Mr. Wickham*!

Unable to accurately match the man to a Regency character, Molly congratulated herself for at least being able to identify the man's uniform. That last trip to the museum in Moscow had been worth the price of entry. *Prince Charming* appeared to be with the Imperial Russian Horse Guard Regiment. His white wool tunic was complete with gold bullion fringed epaulettes, and a silver bullion braid of orange and blue trimmed the collar, front, and cuffs. It was a resplendent example of a dress uniform. Molly had to restrain herself to not ask permission to inspect the gold toned, double-headed eagle buttons, as she gently tapped Leah's shoulder.

"Oh, here you are, Marina," Leah purred. "I was worried we lost you."

"Yes. I can see you are concerned," Molly replied dryly. "It's written all over your face."

"Yes, well—Miss Marina Davidovich, may I introduce you to Lieutenant Dmitry Yegorov... Marina?"

"Yes—oh yes. Pardon me." Molly brought her eyes up from the exquisite detail of the man's buttons to look instead at the man's eyes. "Good evening. It is a pleasure for you to meet me—uh, excuse me—to meet you, I mean..." *Get a grip Molly!* "It is a pleasure to meet you, Lieutenant Yegorov," she finally was able to say.

With a snap, Dmitry Yegorov stood at attention, clicked his heels together, and performed a brief bow. He then turned slightly and lowered himself to whisper in Leah's ear. This caused Leah to bring a gloved hand to her lips, giggling and blushing like the ingénue she was. Without further comment, the lieutenant turned and walked away.

Molly waited for some sort of explanation, but realizing none was to be offered, she came to the conclusion that Lieutenant Dmitry Yegorov was rude and Leah was clueless. He was definitely a Mr. Wickham.

"Oh, calm yourself, Marina. I can see that you are ready to burst! Do let me explain. Dmitry paid me a lovely compliment and then asked permission to introduce his companion, Lieutenant Sergei Pavlenko. I am certain that he will be quite agreeable and that you will find him to be a charming partner."

"Partner? Oh no. No way! You are not going to pawn me off that easily. And I am not dancing. I don't know how—Leah, I told you. I don't know the steps. I..."

"Ladies," Dmitry Yegorov interrupted, "please allow me the honor of introducing my good friend, Lieutenant Sergei Pavlenko."

Lieutenant Pavlenko bowed with great ceremony and reached for each lady's hand. "I am enchanted. What beauty! It is a great pleasure to meet such lovely ladies. The pride of Mother Russia! I will treasure this moment long after the evening has come to an end."

Quickly identifying the man as a fool, Molly removed her hand from the lieutenant's firm grasp. She was uncomfortable with his flowery speech, but unsure how to proceed in the conversation without showing her derision. Seeing Leah, flustered and bubbling with excitement, only gave her cause for regretting the evening entirely.

"Come. Let us partake of some refreshment. There is a lovely array of sweets and champagne in the adjacent room," Dmitry Yegorov said, as he offered his arm to Leah.

Without waiting for a reply, the two walked away leaving Molly alone with Lieutenant Pavlenko. The orchestra was starting a new piece. Couples were forming on the dance floor. Molly knew what was coming next. The lieutenant bowed with great flair.

"Would you do me the honor of partnering with me, Miss Davidovich?"

"Thank you, but no. I—I um, I think I would enjoy some champagne. Why don't we join Leah and Lieutenant Yegorov?"

"As you wish, But, of course!"

The peacock of a man performed another elaborate bow; his right hand was placed over his heart, his left waving about in the direction of the sweets table.

Molly allowed the lieutenant to place her hand on his forearm as he led her to find Leah. *Pavlenko*? Ha! More like *pavote*. Molly rolled her eyes thinking of the Argentine slang term for a fool.

The desserts and other refreshments were laid out in an extravagant display. The room, decorated in cream and gold tones, was the perfect backdrop for the multicolored petit fours, cakes, fruits and rich custards. Molly scanned the room as Pavlenko handed her a delicately etched champagne coupe, which she gladly accepted.

Upon taking her first sip, she caught a glimpse of Leah's cream chiffon slipping behind a massive column. Handing her glass to Pavlenko, Molly marched across the wide expanse with a terse, "Excuse me" absentmindedly blurted over her shoulder. She hoped he wouldn't follow, but of course, he marched along behind her.

Molly pushed aside the heavy velvet drapes covering the exit to the balcony, and there she found her great-grandaunt in the arms of the lieutenant.

"For heaven's sake, Leah! You promised me..."

Dmitry Yegorov immediately released the young girl who had momentarily become speechless. "My dear Miss Marina, please forgive me," he declared. "I take full responsibility. Miss Leah is a complete innocent in the matter."

"Complete innocent my a..." Molly stopped herself. "Leah, you promised me that we were simply coming to dance. Don't you realize what kind of trouble you are asking for, sneaking out here... with him?"

"Dance? Yes, yes! Of course! Let us join the others on the dance floor," Pavlenko exclaimed, all the while winking at Dmitry and cocking his head in the appropriate direction. "Yes, you too Miss Davidovich. I will not take no for an answer. I must insist!"

Lieutenant Yegorov took immediate action, and pulled Leah behind him as he led her to ballroom. Leah looked behind to see Molly's displeasure, but followed her lieutenant willingly—happy to escape further embarrassment.

"Miss Davidovich? Shall we?"

In shock due to the whirlwind of activity, Molly allowed herself to be led to the dance floor. Instinctively placing her hand on the lieutenant shoulder, she felt his arm encircle her waist when she finally became cognizant of her predicament.

"Lieutenant Pavlenko, please forgive me, but I..."

It was far too late for further explanations; the conductor waved his baton and the musicians complied. A waltz was presented for all to enjoy. All, that is, except for Molly. *How do I get myself out of this mess? Uh...think of Beauty and the Beast! One—two—three, one—two—three.*

"Miss Davidovich, you are quite charming."

"There is no need for flattery, Lieutenant Pavlenko." *And don't talk to me. I'm concentrating. One—two—three. Think of Anna and the King.*

"Do I detect an accent?"

"Um—yes, I am from Lvov." *One—two—three, one—two—three. Think of Maria and the Captain!*

"You dance divinely, Miss Davidovich. Pray, why ever did you reject me at first?"

"I—uh—I am not accustomed to this pastime. I don't dance at home." *One—two—three, one—two—three...*

"Of course, you do not dance at home," said a familiar voice from behind. "Your papa has forbidden it, to be sure!"

Molly immediately released Pavlenko and turned to see an impassioned, and bitterly irate, *Avram Abramovitz!*

"Where is Leah? Where is she?" he bellowed.

Lieutenant Pavlenko came between the enraged interloper and his dance partner, not certain of what was unfolding. Molly tried to push the soldier aside to no avail. Trying to locate Leah among the couples swirling about the dance floor, she attempted to defuse the situation from a rather disadvantageous position.

"Avram, please, calm yourself. Leah is quite well. She is in this very room. Let me find her for you and we will all have a nice chat."

"Woman, do not presume to instruct me! I do not need your assistance in this matter. I knew you would be trouble from the moment I saw you, and here you are, dancing in the arms of a strange man. And where is my sister? I imagine the girl is also conducting herself in this most inappropriate manner."

"Sir, please allow me to introduce myself," Pavlenko interjected. With a bow and a click of his heals, he added, "I am Lieutenant Sergei Pavlenko of the Imperial Russian Horse Guard Regiment. We are all ladies and gentlemen here. Nothing inappropriate has transpired."

"It is forbidden, I say!"

Turning around in circles, Avram scanned the room until finding his sister. Fortunately, Molly beat him to her, as she spotted Leah only a moment sooner.

"Leah, Leah! Come away. Avram is..."

"Avram? What are you doing here?" Leah shouted, and forgetting herself, placed a hand on the lieutenant's arm for support. "How did you know where to find us?"

"You silly girl. Do you think that in a household as large as ours, with so many people about, you could sneak away without anyone noticing? Gitel was in the garden. She informed me that you and Miss Marina slipped out that way—like two scullery maids. Disgraceful!"

"I beg your pardon, sir!" the lieutenant said, finding his voice. "What is the meaning of this outburst? Miss Leah, who is this man?"

"Please, can we all calm down?" Molly pleaded once more. "Let's find a quiet place to discuss this..."

"Miss Marina, I have had quite enough interference from you. You have led my sister astray. She knows this activity is forbidden to her, and to make matters worse, she is in the company of strangers—of outsiders."

"Miss Leah, is this gentleman your brother?" Dmitry Yegorov demanded. "Sir, may I introduce myself..."

"I do not care to make your acquaintance, sir! We are leaving immediately..."

"No, Avram! Please wait. I met this gentleman at the University. Yosef was in attendance. Benjamin and Efraim were there as well. I have done nothing to shame the family. And for the last time, dancing is not forbidden—well, not strictly forbidden at any rate—well, Mama doesn't believe it should be forbidden."

"Miss Leah, I beseech you—will you perform the necessary introductions?" her escort repeated quite firmly.

"Yes, of course. Lieutenant Dmitry Yegorov, allow me the honor to present my brother, Avram Solomonovich Abramovitz," she said, and immediately felt her partner stiffen at her words.

"Abramovitz? Avram, Yosef—Efraim?" he shook his head as if to clear his thoughts. "This talk of shame—of dancing being forbidden? Can it be? Of course. You are *Jews!*" Yegorov spat out the word as he removed Leah's hand from his arm. "Why did you not you tell me? Were you so ashamed?"

"Never!" Leah exclaimed. "How dare you say such a thing? I assumed you knew! You were at the assembly at the University. It was a program organized by Jewish scholars. I told you we had to meet 'by accident' in the book shop. I told you that you could not be received in my home. Whatever did you think?"

The lieutenant responded with a snide, bitter chuckle. "I thought you were a silly, young girl anxious for a romantic rendezvous. And I was more than happy to play along, but I never dreamed you were a Jew. Why if the other officers found out...Pavlenko! I must demand your silence in this matter! I cannot afford for this entanglement to get out about camp. I will have your pledge, sir. After all, you, too, were dancing with a Jewess!"

"Dmitry! I do not understand. How can you treat me like this?" Leah cried.

"Very easily, my dear. It is I who am the injured party. I am humiliated. I have been manipulated into consorting with a Jew! What would my superiors think of me? Especially after some 20,000 Jewish soldiers and their families were banished from Moscow not so long ago. Do not dissemble now. You ought to know the reason why. Your people are not Russian patriots."

"That is utter nonsense. I was born in this country, just as you, Dmitry. Why would you say such a despicable thing?"

"Why, indeed? Your people are useless soldiers. They are unfit for combat. To think that I...Pavlenko! What are you waiting for man? Let us leave this place before my ire truly gets the best of me and I demand satisfaction."

"A duel? Are you insane?" Molly cried out. "Avram—Leah, I think we should leave now."

Taking matters into her own hands, Molly grabbed Leah by the arm and pulled her away—not waiting to see if Avram followed. She was painfully aware that the music had long stopped and the occupants of the ballroom had encircled the quarreling quintet. *This is why I read books—quietly—alone. I can't stand dealing with people and all their drama!*

There was a peal of laughter as the Abramovitz family left the ballroom. The orchestra played on; the music beginning immediately in order to bring the revelers back to the dance floor.

Avram quickened his pace and led the women out of the hotel

to his waiting carriage. Leah, who had been whimpering quietly all along, let loose upon reaching the privacy of the conveyance.

"Do not consider for one moment that your tears will have any effect on me. Disgraceful, impertinent girl! What were you thinking?"

"Avram, I think she has suffered enough. She was only dancing after all..."

"Miss Marina, for the last time, do not interfere in something you clearly do not understand—although for the life of me, I cannot comprehend how this is a foreign concept to you! Furthermore, the issue here is not only the dancing. I am fully aware that in regions where pietism weighs more lightly on the community, a *freylech* might be danced with mixed couples, but this was neither a Jewish community nor a freylech! Leah left the house without permission—without a proper escort! She has been consorting with a man that was not properly introduced to the family. This man is not from our community. He is a member of the Imperial Russian Army!"

"But Avram, we too are Russian." Leah cried out.

"You will be quiet, or you will truly see my rage! Can it be that you have forgotten the story? Our father's nephew, Naftali, was only ten years old when he was kidnapped, or as they say, recruited, as a cantonist. Ten years old and sentenced to serve twenty-five years in the Russian army. Some 70,000 boys lived and died for this army and that...that Casanova dares to question Jewish patriotism! Naftali died in the Crimean war, but even if he had survived the battle, he most certainly would have died of starvation or some other form of foul treatment."

"Brother, must we live our lives based on past tragedies? It is a new world..."

"We have our ways, Leah. We have traditions and *mitzvot* to observe. If we continue on this current path of assimilation, we will have nothing! We will be lost. Look at the chaos in our own home. Brother fighting brother. There is talk of Enlightenment, but at what cost? Where does it end? Our numbers are dwindling in the yeshiva. Our men are emigrating to Eretz Ysroel, not to study, not to serve the community, but for politics."

Molly remained silent during the ride home. She recognized that Avram had touched upon several valid points, and she needed time to mull things over. He voiced his concerns over the Russification of the Jewish community—the abandonment of tradition, beliefs, and values. She knew that this moment in time was crucial for the family. It was crucial for the entire Jewish population.

There would be a massive wave out of Eastern Europe. When all was said and done, close to 800,000 Jews would escape; and yet, how could she know for certain that things would work out well for her ancestors when she couldn't explain her presence amongst them? Would her presence be detrimental to their survival? And if they didn't survive, what would that mean with regards to her own family's existence?

Bobe Malka was waiting in the drawing room, as were the men of the family. A simple tea service had been laid out, but missing were the sweets and pastries customarily on display. Molly observed the stern faces and only hoped that she might lessen whatever punishment was to be dealt out.

"Well then, Leah. Go ahead and tell Mama what you have done," Avram challenged.

Leah threw herself on the divan. A fresh stream of tears began flowing along with a barrage of incoherent words of supplication.

Seeing that neither Leah nor Avram were going to say anything further, Molly decided to provide a brief explanation, hoping her words might soften the edges. She prayed Bobe Malka would see that circumstances were not as dire as Avram made them out to be.

The brothers, divided in their sentiments, were all too ready to give their opinions on the matter; however, Molly was only interested in what her great-great-grandmother would say. It was Bobe Malka's opinion that matter most. Too late, Molly realized just what she had jeopardized.

"I say that in today's day and age, Leah should be allowed to socialize and enjoy the entertainment and various amusements in which other young ladies partake," Ysroel offered. "If we are truly Russian, why should we keep ourselves separate from others in the same social strata? This is exactly why Yosef and our friends organized a series of poetry readings for enlightened modern thinkers."

"Those in the Bund would disagree with you, Brother," said Efraim. "We should have cultural and educational autonomy. Yiddish is our mother tongue; it should be our national language. The Bund advocates that we shun Russian culture, as we are shunned. We are ridiculed and maligned. Leah disgraced the family by wishing to attach herself to one of them. And, I must say, I lay this shame at your feet. You and your Russian poets!"

"It is time for Leah to make a good match. It falls on us, her brothers, to find the appropriate candidate. The sooner she is married, the better for all!" Avram shouted, pumping his fist in the air to drive home his point. "I fear we have not done our duty. We should have been more protective of our sister—especially with this stranger in the house. The two of them always have their heads together. Who knows what Miss Marina is telling her? They keep to themselves. Why, we hardly see them outside of each other's company. Mama, indeed, the fault of tonight's mayhem may very well lay at your own feet. After all, you extended the invitation to this young woman."

"That will do. I have heard enough," Malka uttered in her usual calm tone. "Avram, as usual, you have provided enough evidence to satisfy a judgment in King Solomon's court. Marina, you have given us your point of view of what transpired this evening; however, I would like to hear why you allowed yourself to get tangled in this imbroglio in the first place. Surely you understood the ramifications..."

"You must believe me," Molly implored. "I would never wish to do anything to cause you embarrassment or bring shame to the family."

Leah, sitting on the edge of her seat, allowed a short gasp to escape.

"Leah confided in me and asked for my help," Molly continued. "I initially refused her. I didn't want to have any part of it."

"But you did help her," Avram accused. "It is of little use now to say that you initially refused to come to her aid."

"I only went along with the plan, because..." Molly stopped herself. It wasn't her intention to get Leah in deeper trouble, but the truth had to be revealed. She turned to face the distraught girl. Leah nodded her reluctant acquiescence.

"Go ahead, my dear," Malka gently prodded.

"I went along with her plan, because Leah would have attended the ball on her own. I *had* to go with her, don't you see? She is very strong willed—you all know that. I told Leah that I would accompany her just this once, on the condition that she tell you about her gentleman friend—if she decided to pursue the relationship, that is."

"Listen how Miss Marina speaks! *Her gentleman friend.* If *she* decides to pursue the relationship. Leah is a seventeen-year-old girl—what does she know of gentleman friends and relationships? It is up to us to decide!" Avram decreed.

"I am the girl's mother. I am perfectly capable of deciding what is to be done and I am pleased with Miss Marina's explanation..."

"Mama, what are you saying?"

"Avram, do sit down. Your stomping about is frightening the poor cat and is not helping my nerves, to say the least." Malka stood and took hold of Marina's hands. "I am grateful to you, my dear. You were faced with a difficult situation, but you chose to assist my silly daughter—even at the risk of damaging your own reputation with the family. Heaven only knows what could have happened had you not been there. Leah is silly enough to get herself into all sorts of mischief, and this Lieutenant Yegorov has proven himself to be quite a rogue. I say thank you to Marina Davidovich and Baruch Hashem that everything has come to a safe and tidy end. Leah, I will deal with your punishment tomorrow. Now get yourself upstairs and ready for bed."

Leah stood and looked about the room. All her finery and bravado could not help her childlike aspect in the eyes of her family. She bobbed up and down in a brief curtsey. "Yes Mama," was all she said before making her escape.

"I suggest we all withdraw to our chambers. We have had quite enough excitement for one evening," Malka pronounced, as she set out to retire. "Marina, prepare yourself for an early morning, my dear. We have a full day tomorrow and we will need to be home in plenty of time for Shabbes."

"Yes, Bobe Malka."

The grandfather clock struck midnight just then. It was a rather penitent Cinderella who returned to her room.

CHAPTER NINE

14th of April

It was not the most convenient of times to traipse across town, but Malka Abramovitz was not one to put things off. Bright and early Friday morning, off they went to visit Zeide Solomon's tomb. Leah was under severe restriction during the long carriage ride. Her invitation to join the party would have been rescinded if Avram had had his way, but he acquiesced to his mother's mysterious commands. Duvid kept still and didn't murmur a word, not wanting to risk his grandmother's displeasure.

Reveling in the peaceful interlude, Molly used the time to mentally go through her lists of names. She could see spreadsheets of genealogical trees in her mind's eye. With all the research she and her father had done, they still had many questions.

Her father, Daniel, was born in Argentina, as was his father, Ruben Abramovitz. Ruben was the fourth and final son born to Yosef and his wife, Sofia. Shortly after arriving in Argentina,

Malka and her brood settled in Entre Rios, but at some point, the family separated. Some couples settled in La Pampa and others in Santa Fe. By the time Molly and her father began working on the family tree, they were left with distant relatives who couldn't recall 'whatever happened to...'

When she had reached an impasse trying to locate documents through the Argentine databases, Molly reached out to the Jewish communities in Ukraine and, in particular, Odessa. It had become the prime objective to discover her great-great-grandfather, and now more than ever, she had been happy to put her language skills to good use.

She and her father had been ecstatic when they received a response from the *Chevra Kadisha.* Unfortunately, it was not the news for which they had hoped. In their communication, the burial society named several chapels that most likely housed the information Molly had requested. However, they had heartbroken to read that the specified locations had been desecrated, either during the *pogroms* of the early 1900's or during WWII when the Ukrainian Jewish community was all but annihilated.

Turning her thoughts now to current events, Molly recalled the daily family squabbles she had witnessed during her stay with the Abramovitz family. They were of great concern. The brothers were unwittingly causing a division that, left unchecked, could prove to be dangerous considering the political climate in which they lived. Molly felt torn. She had to fight every instinct to warn them of the upcoming unrest but, she could not expose them to the knowledge of future events. Bobe Malka had instructed her time and again not to reveal information that might affect their future—and she had done a dismal job at keeping to that edict. Molly recognized that she would have to find a way to broach the subject without revealing too many details. She had to keep it simple—generic—*impersonal.*

"Marina, my dear, I do not wish to disturb your silent reverie, but as you can see, we have arrived," Malka pronounced.

"Oh wow! I've been day dreaming all this time—I mean, uh—I apologize for not being a more gracious traveling companion," Molly stammered.

"Nonsense, malyshka. It is quite understandable. Naturally, you have much to think about. Malka nodded and turned to her grandson. "Lend me your arm, sir. I do not wish to fall flat on my face while stepping out of the carriage."

Duvid was more than willing to assist his grandmother and acted quite the coachman for Leah and Molly, as well. Once they alighted the conveyance, Molly looked around and took in the landscape.

A brick wall heavy with ivy enclosed the area, effectively separating the park from a dirt road and the railroad tracks that lay just beyond. They entered the graveyard by way of a side gate and Malka led the way in a steady and assured pace. Molly kept silent as she studied her surroundings. She was well prepared for the grim sight—she knew not to expect a modern-day cemetery with lush green lawns, park benches, and designated pathways.

Spotting a rather elaborate structure sitting atop of a nearby hill, Molly assumed it was the cemetery's chapel. A sign posted at the crossroads between the domed building and the rest of the park confirmed her guess. She was unable to control the gasp that escaped her lips. The chapel was one of the many locations mentioned by the Chevra Kadisha. Despondent, Molly knew that this place would soon be destroyed. She was bound by the arbitrary rules of a time traveler, however, and couldn't utter a word of warning. Luckily, Bobe Malka and the others hadn't noticed her odd behavior. The environment lent itself to solemnity, and they quietly continued on through the forbidding graveyard.

Hundreds of tombstones varying in size and style lay haphazardly across the wide space. Some had elaborate sculptures and others were made of crude stones. Molly took note of the designs and religious symbols and observed that, unlike back home, they were inscribed only in Yiddish or Hebrew.

The threesome steadfastly followed Bobe Malka as she led the way through the sea of markers, turning this way and that, until coming upon a well-kept gravesite situated on the border of a particular section. A cast iron decorative fence surrounded the plot. Molly noticed that there were several stones and pebbles placed atop. She recognized the Hebrew abbreviation *po nikbar* and knew it meant 'here lies...' The remaining inscription was difficult for her comprehend. Bobe Malka came to her aid.

"It is from the first book of Samuel. It reads, 'May his soul be bound up in the bond of eternal life,'" said Malka with a gentle sigh. "Then, of course, his name follows: Solomon Ysroel ben Duvid. We had it engraved in between the symbol of the priestly blessing."

Hearing the full name read aloud, Molly was moved. "Solomon, son of David." She had mistakenly believed herself prepared for such a moment, but the tears caught her off guard. She attempted to get her emotions in check and willed herself to look scientifically at the object of research. But when Bobe Malka affectionately wrapped an arm around her shoulder, Molly, the reserved and methodical historian became Molly, the lost little girl.

"I'm sorry. I don't know why I am crying. It's ridiculous to cry over someone you've never even met. It's not like I had a relationship with this man."

"Ridiculous? I should say not. You certainly *have* had a relationship with this man and with all his family. Why do you spend so much time researching and looking for clues, names, and dates? We are all interconnected through time and the heavens. You have his blood running through your veins. You have his stubbornness too!"

"We don't have much family at home," Molly attempted to explained. "I didn't grow up surrounded by my grandparents and all my aunts and uncles. I've missed that—I've longed for that. I suppose you are right. We are all connected. Researching the history was my way of saying to them: I didn't forget you. Don't forget me."

"Malyshka, please—no more talk of your home life." Malka turned to the tombstone and quietly uttered a few words. When she concluded her private soliloquy, she turned once more. "Shlomo, my love, this is your great great-granddaughter, Moe-li. Bless her with patience and clarity of mind. Illuminate her path so that she may be guarded and guided on her journey."

Molly pulled out a stone she had stored in her reticule. She approached the tombstone and lovingly placed her memento alongside the others. At a loss for words, she shrugged her shoulders and sought assistance from her mentor. "I don't know the proper words to say in Hebrew..."

"Just speak from your heart, my dear."

She turned to face the marker and let out a deep sigh. *I can't believe this is actually happening.*

"Zeide, I am Molly, daughter of David, granddaughter of Ruben, great granddaughter of Yosef. I am here to acknowledge your importance in my life—in all of our lives. I didn't know you, but I...I will always keep you in my heart. You are not forgotten."

Molly stumbled on the last few words. She wanted to shout out a warning to her companions: Guard this place! She ached thinking of the Torah scroll and all the historic records that soon would be destroyed. She wished her great-great-grandfather, and those around him could rest in peace, but blind hatred would soon wreak havoc on this sacred ground. She turned to face Malka as she struggled to stay the ever-growing trepidation.

"I think I remember a portion of a prayer. I found it while researching another family member's grave. Do you think it is alright if I recite it?"

Filled with emotion, and unable to speak, Malka simply nodded her head.

"May Solomon's resting place be in the Garden of Eden," Molly whispered. "Hashem is his heritage. May he repose in peace in his resting place."

"Amen," Malka affirmed.

Molly walked around the fenced plot and took a moment to reflect. She felt relief. She felt *connected*. "I think my mom would have been proud of me today. She would have had me twirl about and embrace the power of the spirits—which I will not do—but I think she would have been happy that I came and spoke to Zeide Solomon. Thank you, Bobe, for bringing me here. I will treasure the experience forever."

The foursome walked towards the carriage, the women's skirts rustling alongside the fallen leaves. Duvid ran ahead expending pent up energy, startling lazy geese into squawking chaos. Leah found her voice for the first time since they arrived.

"Mama, may we stop at Mordachai's bookshop on the way home?"

Molly eyed the girl suspiciously. She couldn't be thinking of another romantic rendezvous? Leah simply stared back and innocently batted her eyelashes. Malka appeared not to notice the exchange and gladly agreed to the slight deviation in their plans.

"This will suit very well. If you could entertain yourselves for a quarter of an hour, I will visit the apothecary. I hear he has received a new shipment of ointments. Duvid, I will leave you to escort the ladies."

The ride back into town seemed to take half as long as the original journey, and with her mind clear of departed souls and tombstones, Molly was able to pay attention as the horse clip-clopped down the lane.

Storybook farmhouses, complete with scalloped, chalet-style roofs and intricate window trimmings, dotted the countryside. The mare's easy gait allowed her to enjoy the vibrant scenery of fields bursting with color and vivacity. Rich black soil produced bountiful harvests of wheat and spring barley. Sunflowers and hollyhocks, wild and overgrown, swathed the farmers' picketed fences alongside the road, silently reminding Molly of her childhood nature walks and bringing home the point 'to stop and smell the roses.'

I should have relished those outings with Mom. When I get back home, we're going on a long hike.

She noticed colorful porcelain jugs hanging upside down on the fence posts and wondered if they were part of another folktale. Her curiosity piqued, Molly asked her companions if they were meant to scare away evil spirits.

"No," Duvid giggled, being the first to reply. "They are just for the people passing by."

As her eyebrows knitted together in confusion, Duvid continued to explain. "They are meant to show that a spring or a well lies on the other side of the fence. It is customary for the farmer to invite travelers to stop and have a drink of cool, fresh water."

"Oh! How quaint," Molly replied, delighted to soak in more of the local charm. "I still think it has the makings of an amusing superstition...you know, something about a water spirit or..."

"Malyshka, do not be so quick to trivialize our folklore or superstitions, as you call them. There is ancient wisdom in the old ways. Whether they came from the wandering Slavs or the dispersion of the Israelites, these beliefs have accompanied us throughout the generations."

"I apologize, Bobe Malka. I didn't mean to belittle the local beliefs," said a contrite Molly, "but I do have a question, if I may change the subject for a moment. Speaking of cultures and traditions, I am surprised to see the family interacting with the Ukrainian neighbors. How is it that you fare so well within the local community?"

"Those in charge of the empire have brought peoples of many faiths and ethnicities to this place," Malka replied slowly and with much thought. "Our family has a good reputation among the *goyim*—the gentiles. We are fair employers and good neighbors. When it comes to individual relationships; you are correct, the family does fare well. There are good people yet to be found on either side of the fence, much like the sweet water that awaits an expectant wanderer. Taken as a whole, however, it is a far more volatile aspect—there is much resentment and distrust. Yet, we all must live together here in the Pearl of the Black Sea; and very much like the cholent in Mrs. Kraskov's pot, we must learn to mix and meld without destroying the interesting flavors and consistencies of the other."

Molly absorbed the words and stored them for further contemplation. As a historian, she knew of the violence and hatred that would grow unchecked among the populace, but it was good to hear that there was still something of worth in this place. There was individual kindness and respect and generosity. Maybe it stemmed from the 'old ways' and not wanting to upset the spirits.

Upon their arrival into town, Bobe Malka, as planned, left the group to attend to her errand. The remaining party dutifully walked down the avenue to visit Mordachai's establishment—Duvid strutting like a proud peacock with two young ladies by his side. Molly took the opportunity to lean over and whisper in Leah's ear.

"I can't believe you had the audacity to ask your mother for anything, let alone, requesting to stop at the bookshop. Just so you know: I'm watching you. I better not see you speaking to any strange gentleman."

"Oh Marina! Do you think so little of me?" Leah said with exaggerated despair.

"I'm just giving you fair warning, that's all."

They reached the shop and entered with some commotion—the girls exchanging biting remarks and Duvid tripping over the dreaded threshold. Leah asked to see the new romance novel and was led to a table that showcased a charming display. Molly watched as the teenager picked up one book, leafed through it, and set it down. When Leah stole a glance over her shoulder, Molly shrewdly pivoted avoiding eye contact and was pleased to find

Duvid entertained with a floor globe mounted on a mahogany, trestle stand.

Turning back around, she watched as Leah walked to a corner unit, and from her vantage point, Molly was able to read one or two titles on the shelf: *Le Follet Courier des Salons, Journal des Dames et des Modes.* She laughed. Fashion plate periodicals? Leah was reading the current issue of Vogue.

Satisfied that the teenagers—*her ancestors*—were behaving, she allowed herself to peruse the books of various notable authors and titles. Under normal circumstances, Molly would have been in seventh heaven surrounded by such fine work, but something unusual caught her eye. On a side table, near the back of the shop, Molly zeroed in on the time-honored and familiar words: Baron Maurice von Hirsch.

It seemed that a stack of handbills had been purposefully placed out of obvious sight. Had the shopkeeper wished them to be prominently displayed, he would have placed them by the door, or next to the cash register, she reasoned. Wanting to be discreet, she casually flipped through a newspaper before finally picking up a flyer. She quickly scanned the first paragraph:

Baron Maurice von Hirsch created the Jewish Colonization Association on September 11, 1891. Since then, the agency has surpassed expectations. On Tuesday next at 6:00 in the evening, you are invited to attend a non-political meeting. Come hear more about the flourishing agricultural colonies in Argentina. Learn how you can join your compatriots in the 'New Jerusalem.'

As she cast her eyes from side to side—checking on Duvid and Leah—Molly found herself looking straight at Yosef Abramovitz. *Not again!* She quickly folded the flyer and tried to hide it behind her back. She wanted to take it home and read it thoroughly.

"Good afternoon, Miss Marina. Has Mama allowed you an outing on your own?"

"Good afternoon," she replied. "I am not alone. Leah and Duvid are with me. Your mother will be joining us shortly."

"It is unusual to see you unattended. Mama is usually at your side, if Leah is not clinging to your arm. Even Duvid seems to be your champion. Have you found anything of interest, here in Mordachai's little shop?" Yosef said, attempting to portray only mild curiosity. "I am sure you have quite a selection of literature at home."

Molly couldn't seem to stop fidgeting. She began playing with the strings of her reticule, and forgot that she was trying to hide the flyer behind her back. "I find that Mordachai has an impressive array of titles, more than enough to interest a simple girl from Lvov," she offered.

"Ah, but you are not just a *simple* girl, are you? I see that you have found something more tantalizing than a romance novel or Russian poetry. A leaflet of some sort? Advertising a ball perhaps, or a play...ah, no. Not at all," Yosef said, as he gently pulled the flyer out of Molly's hand. "Baron Hirsh and his Argentine colonies. Does this interest you, Miss Marina?"

"Well, yes—to be perfectly honest—yes. I find it very interesting."

"Why should you care about emigration?"

His line of questioning put her on the defensive. Molly was uneasy as she replied. "I didn't realize that you cared about my interests, Yosef, but since you ask..."

"You are a peculiar creature. Maybe Avram was right about you. I cannot put my finger on it, but there is something unusual about you and your visit." Yosef suddenly lowered his voice and leaned in to whisper in her ear. "What are you truly doing in Odessa, Miss Marina—if that is your real name? I do not believe that your father is a business associate of ours."

Yosef took hold of Molly's arm and lead her behind a curtain to a small, meeting room. "Come now, madam," said he, "what are you hiding and why has my mother come to your aid?"

Disentangling herself from Yosef's hold, Molly busied her hands with straightening her skirt. She didn't trust herself to look directly in his eyes. *He couldn't possibly have figured out the truth!* She didn't have confidence in her abilities to talk her way out of this situation—she was never any good at spontaneous comebacks. If only Yosef would give her fifteen minutes, she'd come up with something clever.

"Since you refrain from replying, allow me to explain my position," he continued. "You have now heard me argue with Avram and my brothers on several occasions. We all are frustrated and anxious, so much so, that we are constantly at each other's throats. We are seeking some sort of release, each of us in our own way. Avram clings to tradition and prayer and the old ways. I look ahead and see a different world. I have been researching various groups, the Bund in particular, but not exclusively. I find that I cannot agree with many of their policies, but you, Miss Marina—well, to be frank, I have come to the conclusion that you are on some sort of mission. Perhaps you are with *Po'alei Zion*. Are you are a Zionist or, heaven forbid, a Marxist?"

"What? You think I am some sort of spy?" Molly said, her voice mixed with relief and nervous amusement. "Let me put your mind at ease. As well you know, the original Po'alei Zion group of Minsk didn't agree with Marxist ideology, *nor do I*. Now please, let me ask you a question, Yosef. You say that you are looking for a new way of life. Have you considered Eretz Ysroel or this so-called, New Jerusalem in Argentina?" she asked, unfolding the handbill.

"Truth be told, I have considered many things, but mostly, I consider that *this* is my home. My father built a successful business here. We have friends and family here. Why should I leave? Because I am a Jew? Why shouldn't I speak Russian and Yiddish? Why shouldn't I mix my Jewish heritage with my Russian culture? Why must I leave and start all over again?" Realizing his voice had reached a fevered pitch, Yosef moderated his tone before continuing. "Miss Marina, is it possible you are working with an underground movement? I have heard of these groups using young woman to spread their message. Maybe you are trying to infiltrate our factories and speak to our workers?"

"Yosef, really! You are not making any sense! I've read in the newspaper that your factories are clean and well maintained. Your employees are paid a fair wage and are treated decently. Why would *your* mother be assisting me to organize your workers against you?"

"I do not know how to respond to you. You know of such things that would turn most young ladies red with shame. I…that is to say…well, I find my life is a chaotic mess! Sofia is relentless with her plans and I…"

"Sofia? She is already in the picture?" Molly said, jumping at the mention of her great-grandmother's name.

"What do you mean, *she is in the picture*? Is this a common saying in Lvov? Do you know Sofia Feinstein?"

Too late, Molly realized that she misspoke—again. *I just need to keep him talking. Maybe he'll forget about my quirky Galitsyaner vocabulary.*

"What does Miss Feinstein have to say about the matter?" she asked.

"What does she say about the matter? She does not speak of anything else! Sofia's father has mysteriously disappeared. He has been missing since *Pesach*. She has mentioned Baron Hirsch to me several times, and as soon as we find her father, she wishes us to marry and leave this place," he stopped short, realizing he had said too much.

"Disappeared! But why?" Molly exclaimed. "Yosef—please. You must believe me. I am not your enemy. What has been done to find him?"

"Naum Feinstein is a member of the Bund, or rather, *was* a member. He began having trouble with the organization when he started spouting Zionist philosophies. We—my friends and I—have been looking for him for the last month. We think the police have taken him for questioning. They are most likely trying to infiltrate Jewish, 'rebel rouser' organizations. I have been following a certain low-level police officer. I believe he will lead us to Naum."

"But Yosef, how will you manage to speak with him? You must think this through very carefully. What are the ramifications if you question the officer?" Molly asked, terrified at the thought.

"I have been trying to meet him casually, as if quite by accident. I thought I could strike up a conversation and see where it leads," Yosef replied. "I organized the poetry reading at the University in order to attract him and his friends into our circle. I almost caught up with him once when I was out running errands with Leah. I had to leave her abruptly in a tea room while I followed his trail, but unfortunately, I lost him. Then another opportunity arose at the public ball. You will recall—when we met quite unexpectedly—I told you that I was there to speak with someone."

"Poor Miss Feinstein!" Molly cried. "She must be out of her mind with worry."

"Naturally, Sofia is frightened. She is frightened for her father, and for their future here in Odessa—for *our* future."

"And you disagree."

"Yes! As I said, I do not wish to leave like a dog with his tail in between his legs. I have done nothing to elicit such contempt from my countrymen. Such mistreatment! My father would not have wished us to abandon our home and our business. He was a well-respected man within the community."

"On the contrary! Bobe Malka stressed upon me that the family's safety was of the utmost importance to your father. Why else would he insist having you all under one roof?"

Impassioned, Molly forgot herself and reached out to grab Yosef's arm. She knew she had to take advantage of this private moment. "And tell me Yosef, why would the family honor his wish of remaining together after all these years? Your older brothers and sisters could have moved away and formed their own households by now. But they haven't done so because nothing is more important than one's family. Not the business—not anything."

Molly looked at the flyer in her hand, now crumpled and torn. She gazed upon the young man who would be her great-grandfather and took a leap of faith.

"Baron Hirsch is offering a new beginning—a new chance on the Argentine plains. If your father could build a textile empire here in Russia—under these conditions—imagine what you and your brothers could accomplish in a free and open society. I—um—

I have read about the success of the Jewish colonies established by the J.C.A. Each family is given a homestead, some animals..."

"And what do we know about this kind of life? We work with silks and brocades. Our livelihood is based on the production of textiles for heaven's sake, not cattle or wheat. We are used to a cultured life, surrounded by books and theater. The J.C.A. is not a gift sent down from Mount Sinai, Miss Marina. The colonies are not the answer to everyone's needs. What are we to do on the plains of Argentina?"

Molly was well versed in the traditional Jewish gaucho saying: We sow wheat and reap doctors. She also knew that the first generation of pioneers would suffer greatly.

The Jewish Colonization Association did not begin functioning a well-oiled machine. There would be many failures due to mismanagement, greed, and politics. Yet, there would be great success in the end. The colonists, as the Jewish settlers were called, would sow wheat, corn and barley. They would tend to the land and the animals, but they would also succeed in building schools, hospitals, and theaters. They would reap doctors, lawyers and teachers and they would live in the great metropolitan cities of Buenos Aires, Cordoba and Santa Fe. If indeed the J.C.A. was not God's gift to humankind, there could be no doubt that it was a gift for the Jewish people of Russia and Eastern Europe.

They simply had to leave Odessa. The next wave of pogroms would soon start, and even if the Abramovitz family survived the Russian Revolution, darker days awaited with the advent of Hitler and the Nazi war machine. Bobe Malka warned her time and again that speaking of future events was a perilous act. Of course, as a historian, Molly realized she was taking a great risk, quite possibly altering their future and her own, but how could she keep silent?

Before having a chance to utter another word, she heard Bobe Malka's voice coming from the front room. Her mother, Judith, would have called it divine intervention; Molly took it as an opportunity to redirect her thoughts.

"Yosef, I do not wish to upset your mother. Please refrain from questioning her," Molly begged. "I wish I could say more, but I am not at liberty to do so. I promise you that I am not here to cause any trouble to you or your family. If it is any consolation, please know that I hope to be gone soon." She left the flyer on the table next to the others, not wanting to risk taking it home. After all, Leah might find it and Molly didn't want to have to answer any more questions.

Walking to the front of the store, she fidgeted with her gloves and appeared overly concerned with smoothing out her skirt. Malka took one look at her and noticed she was flustered. Out of the corner of her eye, she noticed Yosef as he came from the back room—the same room from which her young charge exited.

"What has happened, Marina?" she asked quietly.

"Nothing, nothing of consequence. Yosef and I were just talking, but ..."

"Malyshka, we have already been greatly affected by your presence." She waved her hand for silence as Molly began to object. "I believe you, my dear. I also believe that we need to get you home as soon as possible. Whatever the reason you have traveled here, it is time for you to return."

Malka called out to her children. Leah and Duvid quickly appeared. Unbeknownst to the party, Yosef tucked a flyer in his back pocket and left the shop before his mother could question him. Molly followed dutifully as they walked back to the carriage. Adjusting her black silk caplet, Malka noted that it was becoming rather chilly. She requested a blanket for her lap, which the coachman readily supplied.

"I am looking forward to our tea, children, and perhaps a quick catnap before Shabbes. What say you malyshka?"

"Yes, that sounds lovely," Molly acquiesced. She was quickly learning that arguing with Bobe Malka was fruitless. Her long-standing reputation for being spirited and tenacious was vastly underrated.

Once at home, Duvid was dismissed and sent off to his own mother's care. Leah was sent to her room with a reminder that her tutor was expecting a completed essay by Monday morning. Molly, invited to take tea with her great-great-grandmother, was thankful that the parlor was empty. The others had already had their refreshments.

"I didn't realize I was so hungry," said Molly. "I can't get over the amount of food that is served in this house. It's like a buffet. It's never ending. And the variety!" she exclaimed as she picked up a delicate morsel. "I'm so relieved that we are not eating borsht and herring every day."

"We ate borsht and herring every day for many years, my dear. In fact, that would have been considered a luxurious meal in my youth," Malka chuckled. "Sometimes, we ate potatoes three times a day. We could make a meal with a boiled potato and a bit of herring. Or a baked potato in its skin—the skin has nutrients, you see. We ate potatoes with fried onions or potato latkes or potato knishes. Of course, we also made potato kugel, and during the harshest of times, we used the water of the boiled potatoes to make soup."

Malka placed a sugar cube in her mouth, held it with her teeth, and delicately sipped her tea. "Gitel knows of what I'm speaking," she said nodding to the girl standing quietly in the corner. "You were raised on boiled potatoes, weren't you, my dear? Baruch Hashem, we may enjoy other delicacies today. That being said, if ever the day comes where we need to economize, I will know how to feed my family. One must be prepared to face life's challenges as they present themselves. You cannot plan for every event."

Molly kept silent at this last remark. She knew what hard times the family would have to face on the *pampas*. They would have to make do with Bobe Malka's watery potato soup for quite some time, and the luxuries of home would be replaced with a wooden shack and a dirt floor. But they would be together. They would praise God and be grateful that they were safely away from rioting mobs and revolutionary zealots.

Bobe Malka's last remark had not been lost on her: *You cannot plan for every event.* That was something Michael would have said. With not a little shame, Molly quietly finished her tea, realizing once again, her great-great-grandmother had taught another life lesson.

CHAPTER TEN

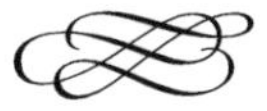

17th of April

Saturday, after Duvid had spied three stars shining brightly in the evening sky, the family celebrated Havdalah with the scent of sweet spices and the glow of a braided candle. It was a special treat for Molly as she had rarely experienced the ceremony with much regularity. Havdalah brought memories of summer camp and singing Debbie Friedman songs around the fire. It brought to mind special holidays, such as Yom Kippur when, after a day spent in prayer and introspection, everyone was filled with the sense of tradition and optimism.

She knew that for this family, who celebrated Havdalah on a weekly basis, it was just as magical. It was not something they did by rote but rather, with enthusiasm and sanctity. They separated from the holiness of the Sabbath and prepared for a new week with renewed faith and it was this faith that caught Molly's attention. They always were looking ahead, going forward—not necessarily with a plan, but with hope.

As the previous week, the days quickly fell back into a coordinated, if not comfortable, routine. Molly had begun to understand the specific times for meals and tea. There were organized preparations for dressing which, of course, were dependent on whether they were going into town or preparing for dinner. She was catching on to the delicate, sort-of choreographed, ins and outs of keeping polite society. Mostly, she eagerly waited for an opportunity to search for the mysterious Queen, but each outing with Bobe Malka had to be orchestrated in such a way as to not appear suspicious.

On Sunday, they managed to go into town with the excuse of visiting the library and the orphanage. The truth of the matter was that they actually traipsed across the village and out into the deep woods to call on a *Babe Yaga*-type rustic. She was an unruly looking woman with an enigmatic air about her. Bobe Malka was certain that she would be able to assist them in their search for the Queen of Eight Wands, but they were sent away empty handed. Rather than disappointed, Molly was somewhat *relieved* at their abrupt dismissal, for the old woman became suddenly incensed, ranting and raving about the inappropriate manner with which they approached her. She continued to curse them as they abandoned her wooden hut with great speed.

"Behold! Ye who are lost, are on a hopeless quest. Ye are not prepared to receive my guidance! Look to ye spirit first!"

Molly couldn't remember when she had been so frightened. A hopeless quest? Was she doomed to live out her life in the wrong century? And what did the crazed woman mean: look to ye spirit? *What is wrong with my spirit?* It took her the rest of the afternoon to stop reliving the scene which had so vividly reminded her of a Halloween outing gone desperately wrong.

The following day, they used the museum and touring the factory as justification for another outing about town, but not before experiencing a rather thought-provoking interlude brought on by none other than her great grandaunt. Leah had been sent to provide Molly with another ensemble for the outing. The elegant bustle dress showcased a dense pattern of violets springing from a bed of winter green vine leaves. The jacket bodice and skirt of jacquard were complimented by mother-of-pearl buttons at the collar, cuffs, and hem.

Leah fussed with the sleeve, straightening the dark green satin trim and adjusting the neat stitches which created the honeycomb detail. She absent mindedly mentioned that the dress was one of Rivka's favorite's as the material had been an inspiration from the Victoria and Albert Museum in London. Molly took note of the location and questioned her further.

"On occasion, Papa had traveled throughout Europe with his own father," Leah explained. "Business trips to London and other locations throughout England were necessary due to the area's increased production of cotton. Papa was especially eager to attend the Great Exhibition, for there he was able to meet with other manufacturers and textile designers."

"That makes sense," Molly exclaimed. "Prince Albert was a key player in the industrial revolution and a champion of expanding the empire. I remember reading about the Crystal Palace Exhibition of 1851."

"Yes! That is correct," Leah continued. "Although Papa was a young upstart at the time, he profited in these international presentations by making connections with the French and English.

The competition was fierce as manufacturers were eager to provide everything from the least expensive printed cotton to the finest luxurious woven silk. And my grandfather was determined to be the most admirable participant in the game. Indeed, it *was* a game! When France organized its own exhibition in 1855, Papa attended and outbid many competitors. He came home with mountains of material, including the material for this very dress. When he and Mama married a few years later, she insisted on accompanying him on his next expedition. Together, they explored the *Musée des Arts Décoratifs* in Paris, and the *Musée de l'Impression sur Étoffes*, which was the cotton-printing center of Alsace."

"The French couldn't be outdone by their neighbors, could they?" Molly said with an impish tone. "Naturally, they wanted to match, or better yet, outshine the Victoria and Albert Museum. And Bobe Malka—what a go-getter! She *would* want to be in the thick of things."

"Precisely so! And Papa was terribly excited to learn about the new techniques of printing. He was able to implement many of these concepts here in our factory, and this allowed the business to grow immensely. Moishe was trained in all of the new mechanical techniques, and soon, he was successfully printing a wide variety of textured fabrics. This was of great importance, as you can imagine, as it was no longer necessary to import textiles and Papa could concentrate on the export market."

"I am very impressed, Leah. Not only are you knowledgeable about your history, but you show a deep interest in the family's business."

"Mama has trained us well. We each of us, Sara, Rivka, and I have a good understanding of color, textile, and fashion. I enjoy the fashion aspect and—I will let you in on a little secret—Moishe has been allowing me to study the fashion plates we have imported from France! He intimated that one or two of my own designs might do very well for next year's production. Can you imagine?"

"That is wonderful news! I have to admit that I've never really given fashion a second thought. I normally pick something off the sales rack, and if it fits, I buy it. I never thought about someone designing a look or cutting a pattern. It would never have occurred to me to think about the process of manufacturing this cloth. Why, just look at this dress. It is in remarkable condition, considering when the material was purchased."

"It was only just made last season. You see, we have stock piles of bolts from Papa's trips. He had tremendous vision. He knew that the time would come when leaving the country would prove to be difficult due to war or heavier restrictions placed on our community. The material was woven by a powered jacquard loom. The gown owes its longevity to the machine that produced the fabric and to the seamstress that fashioned it. It is top quality, to be sure."

"I would never have thought to hear you speak like this, Leah. I wouldn't be surprised if you were the next Coco Chanel!"

"I beg your pardon?"

"Oh, sorry! Never mind!" Molly said with a nervous laugh. "My mind is turning into mush; I can't seem to remember to keep my modern references to myself. Just let me say that I hope you continue in this vein. With your background and your good eye, I wouldn't be surprised to find out that you made a real name for yourself."

"But I do have a real name—Leah Solomonovna Abramovitz —remember?"

The girls were laughing and primping in front of the mirror when Malka walked in the room. She felt a sense of pride and gratitude in seeing the two of them together, and yet, she knew that a heart wrenching parting was only days away.

"Well, this is a pretty sight," she said. "Are we at last ready to depart? I should like very much to return home before dusk and at this rate..."

"Never fear, Mama. We are ready."

"Very well. Do make haste. There is a particular person that I would like to meet; and as I understand it, she occasionally leaves early to attend her ailing husband."

"Who might that be?"

"A young woman by the name of Raisa Ginsberg. Are you acquainted with her?"

"Yes, I believe so," Leah replied. "She is from Bialystok, is she not?"

"She and her husband lived in Bialystok, but their families were originally Prussian. They come from a long line of weavers. It was one of the reasons my dear Solomon hired them almost immediately upon their arrival to Odessa."

"Why is that?" asked Molly.

"They, and many others, were the first families to establish textile factories in an area called Kalisz. They were famous for their embroidery and, indeed, their lacework. Solomon knew that they would be an asset to our compliment of workers. But I am not interested in her lace skills today. I am interested in her knowledge of the tarot."

The girls looked at each other knowingly, and drawled in concert, "*Oh.*"

The trip to the factory proved to be educational rather than beneficial. As Malka had envisioned, Raisa had been given permission to leave early for the day. Moishe, a benevolent manager, had seen fit to excuse the woman from her post. He knew she was caught in between having to provide for her family and needing to nurse her husband. She was an exemplary employee with eyes of an eagle and fingers that worked at lightning speed. Moishe wouldn't risk losing her.

However, Raisa's departure spoiled the opportunity for an impromptu tarot consultation. The resolute trio decided to return home, but not before Malka had a word or two with her son. She had become suspicious of his behavior as soon as they had set foot on the premises. He hadn't invited his family into the office—this was highly unusual.

It was Moishe's custom to ask her to review the quarterly figures or approve a new pattern before it went into production. Something was wrong. Malka didn't hesitate in bringing the matter to his attention.

"What is it, Son? You do not seem quite yourself."

Moishe busied himself with a bolt of cloth and avoided looking directly at his mother before replying.

"It is nothing, Mama. We are extremely busy here today. I do not have time for guests."

"Do not dissemble with me. Out with it," she demanded. "What has happened?'

He knew it was of no use to engage in battle with his mother. Although he was a grown man with children of his own, he acknowledged that Malka Abramovitz was a force to be reckoned with. He respected her mind, as well as her tenacity.

"There is no easy way to say this, Mama. I will, therefore, be blunt. Vandals broke in last night and ransacked the main floor.

They destroyed our newest loom and made off with a substantial amount of money. I had planned on stopping by the bank to make a deposit this afternoon..."

Leah gasped and turned quite pale. Molly waited for the waterworks to begin; however, none came. Malka calmly tugged at her gloves and straightened her silk skirt as she prepared her next command. "Let me by, Moishe. I want to see the damage."

"I would rather you did not come through just yet, Mama. The miscreants have smeared vile slogans on the walls. I have a few men painting over the filth. It will take some time to set things to right."

"Very well," she acquiesced. "I do not wish to have Leah and Marina exposed to such an unpleasant scene."

"Unfortunately, there is more to relate," Moishe admitted. "I notified the police, of course, as soon as I discovered what had occurred. You will be surprised to hear that I received a visit from the commissar himself. He did not seem overly disturbed by the vitriol expressed by the vandals, or the damage they caused. In fact, he intimated that this is just the beginning of what we can expect. There are those who are proposing a special tax be levied on Jewish merchants. Others are calling for businesses to be given over completely to the laborers. He, in point, believes that these acts will curtail further aggression and political upheaval."

"I see," Malka replied solemnly. "We shall bring the matter up at home with your brothers. Afterwards, I believe you should discuss it with our colleagues in the Guild. This is not to be tolerated."

Leah, poor girl, had become dumbfounded by her brother's announcement. Molly too had been silent throughout the startling discourse. She held her tongue when she saw how things were unfolding true to course.

She and her father had known that the family arrived with limited funds to Argentina. They had had just enough to cover their initial expenses. They would not have been able to last the first year without the J.C.A.'s help. When Molly experienced the Abramovitz's grand lifestyle first hand, she knew—according to history—it would be stripped away slowly but surely. She just didn't know when or how it started. Now she knew. It had begun.

Malka agreed with her son. It would be best for the group to return home. Although the girls thought it prudent to remain silent and solemn, Malka grinned and patted Leah's hand encouragingly.

"There, there, my little one. It will all work out in the end. We are not defeated yet! And I refuse to allow the actions of a few hoodlums to terrorize my thoughts or control my behavior. We will have a family discussion, as I mentioned before. We will follow in the tradition of your father and your great-great-grandfather, Marina."

"How so?" the girls questioned in union.

"We will sit down and make a plan," Malka chuckled.

The girls followed suit and allowed their laughter to cleanse the tension that hung in the air. They continued home in peace, each one lost in their own thoughts. With the start of a new week, Molly was facing the possibility of celebrating a third Shabbat with her ancestors. She was torn in wanting to go home and telling Michael of her adventures, but was equally happy conversing with the family and learning all those things that would become the stuff of her history.

The thought of Michael caused her to reevaluate feelings she had taken for granted. He was a good man, a solid man—someone with whom she could build a life. They were different as day and night; but like her parents, the essential things that they shared outweighed the minor, unimportant idiosyncrasies. Certainly, they could learn from one and other. They could grow together.

Molly considered her own behavior and how she was acclimating to her current circumstances—outlandish and farfetched as even her own mother could not have devised. Considering the various events, she was pleasantly surprised at herself. She was dealing with things as they were presented. She was neither hiding nor burying her head in the sand (or a book, for that matter). She was adapting and taking on challenges with a new sense of curiosity and spontaneity. It was like her mother always said, 'You've got to go with the flow.' She laughed at that last thought, for she really didn't have any other choice. *Or did she?*

What if she didn't go back home? Maybe that was what she was meant to do all along. Who else was better suited to shepherd the family to safety? Had she been preparing for this her entire life? She was a student of history and genealogy—who better to return to Odessa just prior to the outbreak of the Russian Revolution? What if the purpose of the Queen of Eight Wands was to bring her back to where she rightfully belonged?

Her mind began racing through the possibilities as she weighed the pros and cons of every potential decision. Again, she recalled Michael's last accusatory remarks, in particular, the comment of not being in control of every situation. Molly had not been able to control the mechanism that brought her here, but she was able to determine her reactions. She had options; she could choose her path while keeping a level head. *At least, I wouldn't run the risk of being scattered throughout time and space in the worm hole again.*

She found it interesting that she was able to joke about the matter. It was definitely not a common trait in Molly version 1.0. But the thought of not returning home and being with her family —*never seeing Michael again*—had her reconsidering. The importance of family struck a chord now more than ever.

She had observed Duvid and the other children of the household as they lived each day surrounded by family. Duvid could not understand the fact that she barely knew her grandparents. She had grown up ten thousand miles away on a different continent! Her yearly visits to Argentina had been her only connection with them, and quite possibly, the impetus towards studying history and creating the family tree. If she couldn't experience it first hand, then she would document it, and ensure the legacy prevailed for future generations.

What she experienced within these walls was a chaotic mass of emotions: love, resentment, affection, jealousy, compassion, disagreements—a psychologist's dream come true. And yet, at the end of the day, any child in this household knew that a grandmother's cookie along with a kiss was always available, a grandfather's story was just a moment away, and a multitude of cousins were continually ready for play or mischief.

She, on the other hand, had grown up an only child. And while it was true that her home was filled with love, she had missed the noise and commotion, the family squabbles, the warmth of acceptance—the intimate understanding of one another that only comes with actually coexisting on a day-to-day basis. As never before, Molly was at a cross-roads. She couldn't see a clear path. Should she attempt to return home or should she remain?

One way or another, she needed to gather more information on the Jewish Colonization Association and find a way to bring it to the family's attention. In her short stay, she surmised that the family hadn't yet realized the dire situation ahead of them. The division between the brothers was based on politics and varying degrees of religious observance, but it was not necessarily focused on the urgent need to emigrate. She was determined to attend Tuesday's meeting advertised on the handbill.

Taking a page from Leah's book of deviousness and guile, Molly devised a plan. She would slip out of the house on the evening of the public gathering. Naturally, she would need to find the proper attire, for one simply did not go into town in one's morning frock. Reaching into her wardrobe, Molly picked out what she thought would be an appropriate afternoon walking gown. The blue silk was her new favorite, although, that term had become a running joke between Molly and Leah as each new dress toppled the previous top contender. She had grown accustomed, in a short amount of time, to donning one ensemble after another while Leah pulled and prodded on ivory buttons and multicolored ribbons.

This gown had a gold net bodice, the chiffon ruffled collar was edged in lace. Elbow-length silk sleeves were trimmed in royal blue piping with sky-blue embroidered tulle charmingly peeking out from under the silk. Complementing the silk skirt was an underskirt of ivory chiffon. Molly had decided that every girl should have something of chiffon in her closet. She chose to take the parasol Leah had insisted on leaving behind. It seemed pointless to carry around the flimsy concoction at first, but she had warmed to the idea. The cream satin, with its embroidered detail, seemed to round out the outfit perfectly. With her ensemble coordinated and neatly arranged, she went on to the more important details.

Bobe Malka frequently came to her room in the afternoons, but Molly overheard the mistress speaking with the cook. She would be meeting with Mrs. Kraskov Tuesday afternoon to discuss the contents of the pantry and other vital kitchen issues, thereby giving Molly time for her errand. With that settled, she headed downstairs to the library with a particular book in mind.

A few days ago, she had observed Duvid as he skimmed through the pages of a world atlas. Molly had been pleasantly surprised at his natural curiosity of geography. It was something she previously noted in Mordachai's bookshop when he spent the entire time mesmerized by a floor globe. With more interest in his choice of book rather than its origin, she hadn't asked Duvid for details. The book looked old, but at the moment, it wasn't the most important detail. Today, the date of publication carried a little more weight. The lay of the land would vary depending on *when* the atlas was printed.

She reached the library and found Dvora, Duvid's mother, sitting comfortably by a cozy fire. The women smiled an acknowledgment to each other, but neither struck up a conversation. Dvora returned her gaze to her novel and Molly reached for the atlas—a magnificent example of French workmanship.

Too large for the shelf, the book had been placed on a corner table on the opposite side of the fireplace. Gingerly, she lifted the cover and admired the artistry of the leather binding which had been hand tooled in a rose pattern. She presumed that the burgundy and green hues had been hand painted by an expert artisan and found that the antique brass accents were a charming addition. Molly skimmed over the first few pages of delicate velum. She struggled with the French, but quickly located the object of interest: Date of Publication: 1892.

"Aha! And there it is."

"Excuse me? Did you say something?" asked Dvora.

"Molly giggled. "Please forgive my outburst. I'm just happy to have found what I was seeking."

"In the world atlas? How odd. That happens to be Duvid's favorite book. It was a gift to his father, brought back from Paris by Solomon and Malka."

"What a lovely memento, Molly beamed. "I noticed that Duvid has an interest in geography. This atlas must be a treasured keepsake."

Dvora nodded in agreement. "My Duvid is a boy of many interests, but geography, and in particular, the Americas have caught his attention."

"The Americas? May I ask why?" Molly asked, her heart pounding in excitement.

"The child is fascinated with the natives. When Solomon traveled throughout Europe, he came across a story book of the Wild West. There had been a company touring throughout England, Germany, and France, but perhaps you have heard of a man called Buffalo Bill Cody?"

Molly stifled a laugh and merely nodded.

"Well, they were quite the thing, you know. Everyone was fascinated by the production. My father-in-law brought back a few picture books for the children. Of course, Duvid was very young, but he was Solomon's favorite. The two would spend hours looking at the pictures and Solomon would act out all the scenes. We could hear their laughter all throughout the house!"

"That is a spectacular story. It paints a wonderful picture, but I would never have imagined it. Wild Bill stories being told in the Abramovitz home!"

"Why ever not? All of Europe seems to be infatuated with the golden land of liberty. Being the sentimental child that he is, Duvid cannot help but dream of such a fantastic place, a place where one is free from convention and the political upheaval our people are continually experiencing."

"Dvora, you mentioned that he was fascinated by the natives. I would have thought he'd be interested in the American cowboys."

"No, no, quite the contrary. Ask him—he could talk for hours about the Lakota or the Cheyenne, but I think his favorite subjects —at least, this week—are a group called the Patagonians."

"Oh really?" she gulped.

"Are you acquainted with the name? They are said to be the giants from Argentina," Dvora explained. "He has been diligently reading tales from Ferdinand Magellan's expeditions, as well as chronicles from Sir Francis Drake's circumnavigation. I think the only other subject that holds his attention is the Kabbalah! I would not be too surprised if he found a way to connect both subjects into one."

"That explains why he was looking at this book so intently."

"No doubt. I believe he is studying the Straits of Magellan and the lower provinces of the country. He is a diligent student, my son."

"Is that right? It must run in the family..." Molly smiled as she opened the book and skimmed through until finding South America. Argentina was the leading entry, as the twelve countries of the continent were in alphabetical order. Knowing that the patriots had declared independence from Spain in 1816, Molly had been anxious to see the book's publication date. By 1892, the infant nation would still be going through growing pains, but the immerging provinces of Santa Fe and Entre Rios were clearly defined in the atlas.

Her ancestors were destined to live in these provinces—that is to say, if she could nudge them in to paying attention.

CHAPTER ELEVEN

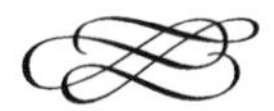

18 of April

On the day of anticipated meeting, the pomp of the morning rituals seemed to take longer than usual. Molly was fidgety throughout breakfast, and on more than one occasion, there were raised eyebrows and silent disapprovals cast her way.

Her first offense had been choosing the wrong spoon. That might have been overlooked, however, she unceremoniously dropped the utensil which upset a delicate plate of sculptured butter.

When she successfully selected the proper piece of silverware, she stirred her coffee so vigorously the dark liquid spilled onto the lace tablecloth. Molly, of course, immediately tried to sop it up. Unfortunately, her only recourse was to use an embroidered, linen *serviette.*

Possibly her worst offense came about as she nervously folded and unfolded the newspaper once too many times—effectively ruining the perfect crease that Oskar, the footman, had painstakingly created for Avram. She excused herself from the table before causing any further damage.

With not much else to do, Molly took a stroll around the garden, hoping that the exercise would calm her nerves and make her less antsy before the next meal. She needn't have bothered.

At luncheon, the dining room was fraught with tension. This was largely thanks to the brothers quarreling over the news in the morning's paper—the one that Molly had nearly torn into two.

There was growing speculation on the possibility of revolution. Yosef pointed out that the people were becoming increasingly discontent. In the rural areas, five years of failed crops had added to the misery of a beleaguered population only recently emancipated from serfdom. Workers in the industrial regions were complaining of inadequate wages, unsanitary conditions, and harsh disciplinary actions. The recent events at the factory brought that message home loud and clear.

The brothers were so occupied with the barrage of verbal assaults volleying back and forth across the table, no one noticed Molly's continuous, yet insignificant, mishaps. With little appetite, she pushed the food around her plate and begged off the rest of the meal, citing an oncoming headache.

Finally relieved of household obligations, Molly prepared for her afternoon outing. While the others were resting, she stepped out into the hallway and quietly found her way to the attic. She knew Duvid would be happily sequestered in his 'secret reading place'. Knocking softly on the door, she entered the boy's hideaway and found him napping soundly amongst his beloved books.

"Duvid, wake up, sleepy head," Molly said, gently tapping his shoulder. "I need your help."

Rubbing the sleep from his eyes, Duvid stirred and stretched, yawning noisily like a grizzly cub.

"Shh! Not so loud!" Molly exclaimed.

"Miss Marina! What are you doing here?"

"Get up, Duvid. I need you to—to escort me to Mordachai's bookshop."

"What? Now? Shall I get Bobe Malka? Have you found the card?"

Molly felt guilty for fibbing, but she had no other way of getting out of the house. She invented a story about receiving a note from Mordachai. He had a possible lead on an interesting tarot set. It was imperative that she go to the store before someone else purchased the deck. Duvid—wanting to be of assistance and proud to have been asked—immediately stood and was at the ready.

"We must be quiet, Duvid. I—uh—don't want to wake anyone up from their nap. Okay?"

"Yes, okay."

She grimaced "Don't say *okay*. Bobe Malka wouldn't approve."

"Okay—I mean to say, very well, Miss Marina."

They managed to leave the house and make their way to the village. Before entering Mordachai's establishment, she made Duvid pledge that he would not mention the trip into town or anything that he might witness within the bookshop. The boy wasn't sure what the mystery was all about, but he was more than pleased to have a role in the production.

Molly walked with him to a small corner table and asked him to choose a book off the shelf. She instructed him to wait for her and not move a muscle. The child, holding his selection, instantly became rigid.

"I promise not to move a muscle, Miss Marina. Ah—may I move my fingers to turn the page?"

Molly laughed. "Of course, silly! It's just an expression. I don't want you to move away from this corner. Okay?"

"Okay!"

"Duvid..."

The boy clicked his heels together and bowed. "As you wish, Miss Marina."

Molly walked to the back room and pulled aside the curtain to reveal a group of fifteen men and women. Someone had begun speaking; he was explaining about Maurice Hirsch and his philanthropic projects.

"As you may know, the baron began assisting our community in 1882. His donations went to fund the first refugees to Argentina. Understanding this to be insufficient, he offered an exorbitant amount of money to the Russian government for the endowment of a system of secular education to be established in the Pale of Settlement. Our esteemed government officials accepted the money, of course, but would not allow a foreigner, albeit a wealthy and well-known foreigner, control over the administration of the funds."

The man paused and allowed his audience to voice their remarks, sarcastic and rambunctious as they were.

"At that point," he continued once the assemblage settled down, "Hirsch decided to devote his money to an emigration and colonization society, one which would allow our community the chance of establishing ourselves in agricultural colonies outside Russia. He founded the Jewish Colonization Association with a capital of £2,000,000, and in 1892, he presented an additional sum of £7,000,000. Last year, after the passing of his beloved wife, the capital was increased to £11,000,000! You see my friends, now is the time to act! The funds are available. Argentina is welcoming us. The land is vast and the need is great for families to work and populate this new country."

There were excited murmurs of appreciation and the people showed signs of great interest. Molly stood back, not wanting to call attention to herself. She looked about the room and saw Yosef standing in the opposite corner. He was speaking to someone rather intently. Luckily, he was far too busy to notice her.

She inched her way over to the other side of the room, certain that he was deep in conversation and unaware of her movement. When she was close enough to eavesdrop, she picked a tome off a shelf, and nonchalantly, began skimming through its pages. With her nose in the book, she unabashedly listened to Yosef's conversation.

"...Naum is in good health. Now that you have provided the funds to pay for his board and keep, they will release him tomorrow morning. Rest assured, my friend."

"Yes, well—his 'board and keep' is more like a king's ransom, but what is done is done," Yosef muttered. "I am grateful that you were able to act as my middle man. I was unsuccessful in obtaining an audience with the officer in charge of Naum's detainment."

"I said it before, but it worth repeating: you must get Feinstein out of Odessa. A socialist he is not, but he has caught the attention of too many officials. America has begun limiting access because so many of our people are running towards her shores. That may not be an option."

"And my future father-in-law does not wish to emigrate to Eretz Ysroel, although he has been Her greatest proponent..."

"Argentina is the next best thing! Naum will advocate for us

Jews and support the Holy Land from afar. The J.C.A. promises the best of both worlds for a man like Naum. He is not a farmer, but he can work on establishing cooperatives. The colonists will prosper working as one. This is Naum's strong suit. He will be happy there. More importantly, he will be *safe*. You must get him on the next boat!"

The two men shook hands, and Molly took this as a sign to sneak away. She ducked behind the curtain and immediately headed to the corner table where she had left Duvid. Thankfully, he was good to his word. She found the boy, snug in his reading nook.

"Come on, little man. It's time to go," Molly said, grabbing his hand and pulling him up from his chair.

They quickly exited the shop and rushed back home. Duvid, being wired for espionage and intrigue, understood the importance of keeping silent precisely at that moment. He hoped that Molly would divulge some fascinating piece of information when they were safely home. The pair entered the estate by way of the abandoned side gate and old vegetable garden, but when Molly instructed him to quietly disappear to his room, he fell behind and hesitated.

"What is it, Duvid? What's wrong?"

"Miss Marina, I overheard something tonight. May I ask you about it?"

Molly felt the blood rush from her face. She stood frozen, wishing the moment away.

"Duvid did...did you get up from your seat after I asked not to move? What did you hear?"

"No, Miss Marina! No, I would not disobey your instructions. Not after you had placed your trust in me. It was that man, the man in the back room... his voice is like the *chazan's* when the synagogue is full and we are seated in the back. Somehow, the chazan can make his voice reach each one of us sitting in the farthest corner. Sometimes I can feel his bellows in my bones! That is how I heard the man speaking about Baron Hirsch and the Jewish colonies."

"Well—okay, but what did you want to ask me?"

"Miss Marina, will the colonists go to the Land of the Bigfeet? Will they meet the Patagonians?"

Molly sighed with relief. *At least he is only asking about mythical giants.* "Duvid, surely you understand..."

"Yes, I know what you are going to tell me—that Magellan and the others were exaggerating. I read that he wrote in great detail about the giants he encountered. In his native Portuguese, he named them *patagão*."

"But Duvid..."

"I know what you are going to say, but they were spotted again in 1776, this time by the British. Even they said the men were giants!"

"Are you asking me or telling me?" she laughed.

"I suppose I am asking."

"I think it is safe to say that the indigenous people Magellan and Byron were speaking of were the Tehuelches. They were nicknamed Patagonians because of their big feet, and from what I have seen, you have been studying many different journals and already know the answer. They were very tall, probably much taller than the average European, but definitely not giants. To answer your original question, the colonists will not be living so far south. It is not very likely they will come across the Tehuelches."

"Miss Marina, why are adults so eager to dismiss things that they cannot not explain? It is like Bobe Malka always says... there is a difference in between inexplicable and unexplainable."

"I'm all ears Duvid. Tell me."

The boy looked curiously at his friend, somewhat like a puppy that tilts his head back and forth trying to decipher what his master is saying.

"Yes—well, Bobe Malka says 'unexplainable' refers to something that truly cannot be explained, perhaps something for which science cannot provide an answer. On the other hand, 'inexplicable' refers to something that is extremely difficult to credit, something that you find difficult to understand. But just because you might find something difficult to accept, does not mean that it does not exist! Perhaps the Patagonians went into hiding—after their initial encounters with the Europeans—and have not been seen ever since. Perhaps they are gentle giants who mean no harm and only wish to live in peace."

"I guess if you put it that way, you may have a point."

"Thank you, Miss Marina. I have been giving this much thought of late, especially since you are here—and we have no explanation." He giggled. "Do you know if the Jewish colonists will meet the Wichi or the Mapuche? I would envy them so!"

Molly was desperately avoiding the point. The fate of the vast majority of indigenous peoples in Argentina would prove to be fatal—if possible, worse than the North American experience. She wondered if she could sidestep the issue.

"Um—yes. The Wichi, and even the Guaraní, live in North East provinces as well as other parts of the country. Duvid, the colonists will meet people from all over the world. There will be Basque peoples, Italians, Spaniards, German, French—even Welsh. They will live among the gauchos and they will learn many things from one another. Some colonists will be known as Jewish gauchos. They will work the land and tend the animals. They will wear the traditional *bombachas* and carry a *facon*, but they will still be Jews and carry on the traditions of their forefathers."

"But will there be more fighting? Will people be angry? There is so much anger here. People do not like living with people who are not like themselves. Why are people so cruel?"

"Not everyone is like that. There are good people and bad in every population. Your grandmother has taught this lesson, hasn't she? You have to have faith that the good will prevail."

"Miss Marina... do you know what will become of me? Will I be a Jewish gaucho? Will I be friends with the Wichi or the Mapuche?"

"I couldn't tell you—even if I knew," she said, wishing she had a better reply. "You've heard Bobe Malka chastise me on several occasions when I have talked about future events. You and I will just have to live our lives one day at a time and see how it unfolds. It's a mystery! Just like the Kabbalah," she grinned, hoping a little humor would help move the conversation out of the danger zone. "Now, let's get inside before we are found out."

Duvid nodded and quietly turned to leave. He took three steps, looked over his shoulder, and came running into her arms.

"That was quite a bear hug. I love you too." Molly gulped, her eyes swelling up with tears. "Now run straight to your room and wait to be called for dinner."

"Okay, Miss Marina."

"Duuuvid!"

He giggled and ran off. Molly stood in the abandoned garden just for a moment, and as she turned to follow his footsteps, she came face to face with Gitel. *Oh, for goodness sake!*

"I do beg your pardon, Miss. It was not my intention to eavesdrop, but I happened to be getting some fresh air—before assisting with the evening meal, you understand. I beseech you! Please do not report me to Mrs. Kraskov. I did not mean to overhear..."

"Calm down, Gitel. I believe you. What exactly did you hear?"

"I heard the little master speaking of the Jewish colonies. I am familiar with the J.C.A. and Baron Hirsch. My uncle, Baruch Saperstein, suggested that I go to Argentina when my parents died last year. I was afraid to leave Odessa, and so, my uncle found this position for me."

"I see..."

"But now, I hear Master Duvid speaking of the same subject. Can I assume that the family will be leaving? Will I be left behind? Whatever shall I do? My uncle will want me to find another situation, as he and his wife are unable to take me in."

The poor girl is terrified, but this is getting out of control. How do I get myself out of this mess?

"I am so sorry to hear of your troubles, but I don't know the family's intentions," Molly said, gently patting the girl's shoulder. "Gitel—Gitel, please do not tell Avram that you saw us here tonight. It would upset him greatly."

"Oh no, Miss! I would never—I would not have said anything to Master Avram about the other night except he went looking for Miss Leah and was very angry that she was nowhere to be found. He insisted that I tell him if I had seen either of you—please believe me, Miss. I meant no harm."

"I don't blame you for the other evening. Of course I understand. But, tonight...tonight, I took a harmless walk and

Duvid accompanied me to Mordachai's bookshop. Ah, Gitel?" She stopped and braced herself for a response. "Did you hear anything else?"

"No, Miss. I walked away after I realized you were speaking of the Jewish colonies. I am afraid of what is to become of me."

"There is nothing to be concerned about, not just yet. I am certain that Bobe Malka will take good care of you in any event."

"Yes, Miss. Thank you."

"Now I really must get back inside. Will you be alright?"

"Yes, Miss. I will return to the kitchen straight away." With a quick bob, she turned and walked away.

Good Lord! What else could happen? I better not jinx myself.

Without wasting another moment, Molly dashed into the house and found her way back onto the main floor. A quick look at the grandfather clock in the hallway showed that they had been gone for little over an hour. The household would just now be stirring in preparation for the evening's activities. Once again in her room, Molly stared at herself in the Victorian dressing mirror.

Who are you?

What would Michael think of her escapades? She laughed and found she was quite satisfied with herself. She had learned that Yosef was well on his way to seeing his family out of Odessa. Her great-grandmother, Sofia would see to it, no doubt.

CHAPTER TWELVE

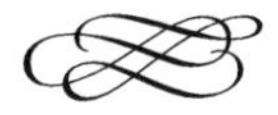

19th of April

Wednesday passed with a flurry of activity. Bobe Malka was unable to tear herself away from her household, as Mrs. Kraskov had twisted her ankle and needed attending. The lady of the house took over without a word of complaint. Meals had to be planned, linens had to be washed, and furniture had to be polish and dusted. Molly was happy to assist, as it allowed her to keep her mind off politics and uprisings, as well as esoteric journeys through time and space.

"It is good to take part in the maintenance of one's home, my dear," Malka said, as she vigorously polished a set of candlesticks. "These candlesticks were a gift to my great-great-grandmother. Her beloved was a well-known silversmith in the village of Trupy. He fashioned them himself and presented the candlesticks to her on the occasion of their wedding."

"Every knickknack is a treasure. There seems to be a story

behind each piece, and I can't begin to explain how meaningful this all is to me. As far as having my own home, I haven't given much thought to it as of yet. I've been focusing on my career," Molly admitted.

"An education is all well and good, but a home of your own—a husband and children—these too are important."

"I suppose that's true, Bobe; but I am finishing my master's degree and I thought perhaps I could attempt to secure a doctorate..."

"Malyshka, my dear heart, this means many more years of study, does it not?"

"That's the thing. I'm not sure what I'll do. Michael has suggested a few ideas. I don't want to choose unwisely. I need time to assess my options before I make a commitment. I...I have been playing around with another idea. It's so ridiculous—I'm just going to blurt it out: What if I stay in Odessa? What if I don't go back and remain here with you?"

"To what end, my dear?" Malka set down the dust rag and gave the girl her full attention. "No, no—I cannot support this new idea. I do not believe you travelled back in time for this reason. What would be the purpose? As King Solomon said, 'A righteous man falls down seven times and gets up.' This tells me that we must move forward. We must live in the moment, learn the lesson, and then move on. And, as my last words on the subject, I do not disagree with continuing your studies, my dear, but do not use one experience to run away from other challenges."

"I suppose the idea of remaining with you was a little 'out there,' but under the circumstances..." She shrugged her shoulders in capitulation. "I guess it's settled then. I'll go back. All I ask is that Mr. Scott beam me back properly."

"My dear, I cannot begin to fathom the meaning of your words."

Molly laughed. "I'm sorry. Don't pay any attention to my prattling. I can't seem to manage to mind my words. But speaking to your original point, I have contemplated marriage. I'm not sure I'm ready just yet. We are still so very young. But these past days away from Michael, I've come to realize how much I miss him. I miss sharing the day's events with him. I miss hearing his observations..."

"*Oy gevalt*! I should have not opened this topic of conversation," said a flustered Malka. "You see, my dear, it has proven difficult for me as well—this necessity to speak of only the present."

A knock on the door disrupted the conversation. Grateful for the interruption, Malka gave her permission for the supplicant to enter.

"Madame, I do apologize for intruding, but Mrs. Kraskov sent me," Gitel explained. "There is a woman asking to speak with you —she is a Ruska Roma. I tried to get rid of her, madame, but she insists on seeing you. I have asked her to wait by the back door."

Molly's interest was piqued. The Romani nomads of Russia were not only known for their horse trading and flamboyant costumes. The Ruska Roma women were famous fortune tellers. She hoped that she would be asked to accompany Bobe Malka to the kitchen. After all, the gypsy might have some information on the tarot card they had been seeking—the card that would presumably send her home. Molly was not disappointed as she, indeed, was invited to join the women.

True to her word, Gitel had not asked the visitor to enter. The Ruska Roma stood at the door, tall and erect with a dancer's slim body. Her skirt, asymmetric tiers of red, orange and gold, swayed about at the slightest movement. Molly admired the *kokoshnik* which crowned the woman's mass of raven curls, framing her face with gold and silver charms. She held her breath, waiting to hear how the mysterious visitor would contribute to their search. Molly watched with pride as her great-great-grandmother approached the gypsy with decorum and hospitality.

"I am Malka Abramovitz. I understand that you wish to speak with me. What can I do for you?"

"My family and I just arrived, madame, and we are living on the outskirts of town. Our tabor is east of the market you recently visited. I was told by a man in the village that you are looking for a particular set of tarot."

"You are correct," Malka conceded. "Will you not come in for some refreshment? We can discuss the matter further."

"That is very kind of you, madame, but I do not wish to cause any inconvenience. I have only come to bring you this deck of cards. The Queen...she is very powerful," said the gypsy as she glanced about the room, her eyes settling on Molly. "She is not meant for the unlearned. Are you certain you understand the ways of the tarot?"

"Yes, and I thank you for your concern. As far as compensation..."

Molly listened as they completed their business. It was surreal; the aristocrat and the gypsy conducted themselves as if it were a common, daily event. A Ruska Romani and her Jewish great-great-grandmother were coming to terms over a tarot card that would transport her back to the 21st century. *How do I rationalize this? I like a good Sci-Fi movie, but isn't this the stuff of paganism?*

Malka handed the woman a bag of coins. The gypsy accepted the payment and signaled to her hidden companions she was ready to leave. Three horsemen approached the back entrance of the house. One man leaned down, and grabbing the woman firmly about the waist, hoisted her upon his lap. Without further ado, they turned the great beasts around, and in an instant, disappeared down the lane. Malka gently closed the backdoor and gestured for Molly to follow. The two quietly slipped into the drawing room where Malka hoped to speak quickly before being interrupted by her curious brood. Naturally, Molly was impatient and full of questions.

"I can't wrap my head around this. Fortune tellers? How is this even close to being acceptable to you? Every tarot card I have ever seen has Christian images—including Satan. How does this mumbo-jumbo make sense in a Judaic environment?"

"Can you not think of Jewish references to the paranormal, my dear?" Amused, Malka allowed herself to chuckle at her great-great-granddaughter's comments. Mumbo-jumbo indeed! "Try to recall the mystifying stories of the Tanakh..." Malka began, but changed course. "Allow me to pose another question. There are twenty-two cards in this deck of tarot. This particular set incorporates Hebrew letters in the design. There are, of course, twenty-two letters in the Hebrew alphabet. Are you familiar with the concept of Gematria? The theory of Hebrew letters and numbers and their powerful connection?"

"Yes, yes—but isn't fortune telling against Jewish doctrine?"

"Judaism doesn't necessarily inhibit the use of 'magic'. The key is how it is practiced, my dear. What began as a tool for contemplation has been corrupted. The tarot was meant to be a mirror of the unconscious. It was meant to help illuminate the path of one who is conflicted. I believe its purpose was not divination, but rather *introspection*."

"I'm suddenly reminded of the Crypto Jews," Molly murmured. "Is it a coincidence that they also had a connection with playing cards? I have long been fascinated by their courage and inspired by their faith and dedication, but I don't believe I ever put all these different pieces together."

"Crypto Jews? My dear, once again the subject of your conversation broaches the edge of a slippery slope."

"But you must be aware of what occurred to the Sephardic Jews during the Inquisition. I am not revealing new information. This is historic data. I read an article which indicated that during the time of the Inquisition, many Jews would secretly gather for prayer by sitting around a table with seemingly innocent cards. If someone came by to spy or question them, it would appear that they were simply playing a game. When left alone, they would return to their prayers. They called the playing cards *barajas*, which refers to the Hebrew word *baracha*—which, of course, means blessing!"

"To be sure, I know of the horrors of the Inquisition and am familiar with the Anusim who were forcibly converted, but the word crypto Jew is foreign to me. Is it similar to the derogatory term, *marranos*?"

Confirming the statement, Molly nodded ferociously. "Yes, the word marrano means pig and it was most definitely meant to be an insult! I have to admit it, Bobe Malka. I am fascinated by the reappearance of these cards throughout history and their ever-evolving significance."

"How do you mean?"

"You have said that the tarot was meant for introspection, and that throughout the ages, the original intent has been defiled. The article I read explained that the *barajas* were not only used as a decoy, but also as a means of contemplation and study. They used the cards to discuss Torah, since they didn't have access to their treasured books. If they pulled a card which contained the image of a king, they told stories of Saul, Solomon, and David. If they selected the number four, they might speak of the matriarchs, and so on. Your views and the information from the article depict a captivating evolution of thought and piety. That's what I meant to say. It's all beginning to make sense and I can see a connection."

"Marina, my dear, you have proven your love of research and history, but I question the wisdom of allowing myself to listen to your discourse. We must not cross the line between your knowledge of the facts and my curiosity and conjecture. We have no idea of the repercussions. Nevertheless, one thing is clear to me. There can be no doubt. There is nothing abstruse about the card we sought. It was neither Cups, Coins, or Swords. It was the Queen of Wands and uniquely—*specifically*—the Queen of Eight Wands."

"Why is that so important?"

"Although she is the Queen, Malka, or Malchut, emanates her strength from the base of the Tree of Life. Her strength sustains you—her power resides in you. I have witnessed this myself: the power to love, to be compassionate, to respect, to teach, to unite, to communicate, to heal and to seek justice. In my opinion, these are *your* eight wands. You only needed to claim them as your own. And now, my dear heart, it is time for you to go home and allow this wisdom to guide you."

Overcome, Molly reverted to a familiar emotion. It wasn't the fear of traveling back in time, it was the dread of separation. Of breaking the connection. "When?" she managed to murmur. "How are we to do this?"

"Do not distress yourself, my dear. Let us have one last meal together, and in the morning, we will ask Duvid and Leah to join us in the attic. I believe tomorrow will be appropriate. You should be back in your world in time to light your Shabbes candles, may it be God's will."

Emotionally spent, Molly returned to her room. It wasn't too much longer when she opened the door to find a teary Leah holding another evening dress.

"I have brought you this gown. Since it is to be our last evening together, I thought you would enjoy something special."

"Ah, Leah. That is sweet, but every gown you have shared with me has been special."

"I will miss you desperately, Marina. Whatever shall I do with myself?"

Molly couldn't help but laugh, and it felt good to bring some humor into the moment. "Well, for one thing, you can try to stay out of trouble."

"Life will be terribly dull without you," Leah cried, sinking down on the bed.

Molly sat down next to the girl and held her hand. She wanted to tell her that life would be the complete opposite of dull! She wanted to tell her to enjoy her posh surroundings, her fancy dresses and lazy days, because soon she might embark on an adventure that would require every bit of strength and courage. But this time at least, she held her tongue. Nothing was written in stone, not their leaving Odessa—not even her arriving safely back home. She wanted her parting words to be on a positive note.

"More than anything else on this strange and miraculous

journey, I've learned that life is what you make of it," said Molly. "Being fearful not only disproves your faith in God, but it shows you don't have faith in *yourself*. Wanting to plan for every future eventuality had me so tied up in knots that I didn't leave any space for the beauty of right now—this present moment. I was so busy thinking of my five-year plan, of where I'd be and what I'd be doing, that I was missing the fun I had in front of my face. And that lack of faith probably goes against a commandment or two—I'd have to ask Avram for confirmation," she giggled. "Like a wise man once said, we need to cherish the moment! And right now, I want to cherish this moment and put on that spectacular gown!"

The girls—great-grandaunt and great-grandniece—stood and embraced. Molly dashed behind the screen and began removing her day dress. The gold damask was exquisite; a blue chiffon sash complimented the gown, cinching at the waist and then draping elegantly down to the hem. She tentatively fingered the beaded fringe across the bodice and admired the intricate gold florets which were dotted with seed pearls. Leah had thoughtfully selected matching gold slippers and gloves to complete the ensemble. Molly twirled in front of the mirror when the last clasp had been fastened.

"It is stunning!"

"You carry it well, Miss Molly Abramovitz. You are every bit a daughter of this house. But I do have a question: Is it your new favorite?" Leah giggled.

"They are *all* my favorites! I wish I could take them with me. Of course, I have no idea how that would work and—even if we could figure that part out—I have no place to wear them. I go around in jeans and T-shirts most days."

"You mean those atrocious things that are hidden beneath your bed? How ghastly!"

"I guess I shouldn't have said that. For the life of me, I don't know why I keep letting these things slip out!"

"You wear them to dinner? To the theater? To the opera? Will you wear them on your wedding day, as well?"

"Leah, I will miss your sense of humor, that's for sure. No silly —I don't wear jeans to the theater, and I haven't thought yet about my wedding dress. I guess I'll cross that road when I get there. That's part of my new philosophy anyway. Now let's go down to dinner, before I lose my nerve."

The two walked down the grand staircase arm in arm, a knot growing in Molly's stomach with each step. *This is my last meal with my family.*

In a moment of desperation, she nearly turned and ran back to her room. She recognized the ache at her core—her throat was already clenching. Molly was no stranger to goodbyes. How many times had she done this before? How many times had she felt her heart ripped to shreds as she said goodbye to her family in Argentina?

Sendoffs were dreaded events. The entire family, grandparents, aunts, uncles, cousins—everyone would come to Ezeiza International Airport to say farewell. Her parents never handled these situations well and their pain—their angst—was transmitted to their daughter. Her mother was musical, and when words failed to express the aching for home and loved ones, she'd often sing the words: '*No soy de aquí, no soy de allá*'... words that automatically would pull at any immigrant's heartstrings. *I'm not from here; I'm not from there.*

Molly remembered a familiar scene that used to play out in her head. On one side, a little demon would whisper: You would have been better off never having met your family. You could have spared yourself this agony. On the other side, a little pixie would whisper: Every experience where you can give and receive love is worthwhile.

Looking back on those scenes as an adult, Molly could now understand her life-long need for security, for stability. She and her long-distance family *had* created special memories; after all, they had relied on those yearly vacations and occasional surprise trips. Her father would joke and thank the heavens for technology —at least they had Skype and social media. It wasn't as if they were waving goodbye from a steamer ship off the coast of the Black Sea. Still, virtual communications or short-term visits were nothing like weaving day-to-day experiences into a communal tapestry, creating family unity through shared events.

After all these years, she knew her Argentine relatives loved and cared for her, but—still and all—she was only a guest in their home. She was a welcomed visitor, one connected by history and bloodlines, but one that had to say goodbye over and over again.

This time, it was worse. This time, she was faced with a bitter reality. This time, goodbye was forever.

All these thoughts swirled through her head as Molly caught sight of her reflection in the majestic gilded mirror at the head of the staircase. A sudden sense of calm came over her. What was it that Leah had said? She was Molly Abramovitz and she was a daughter of this House. The Abramovitz women were made of sturdy stuff. *I am a link in this chain and I will handle whatever comes my way with strength and dignity.*

Although her dinner companions hadn't discovered her true identity, Molly didn't want their last impression of the guest from Lvov to be of a sniveling, clumsy, country bumpkin. She stood her full height, squared her shoulders and took pains to smooth out the imaginary lines of her skirt. Taking a deep breath, she smiled at a concerned Leah as they continued on making an elegant entrance into the grand dining room.

Oskar, the footman, assisted Molly with her seat. This time, she was full of grace and sophistication. No more tripping on the yards of material. No more feeling inadequate in front of the servants. She was daintily adjusting the linen napkin Oskar had placed on her lap, as Bobe Malka began to speak.

"And so my dears, the time has come to say farewell to our charming guest. It has been a ..." she stopped to press a handkerchief gently to her lips. "It has been both an honor and a pleasure to have had Miss Marina in our home. I will forever treasure our time together."

Molly stood and turned to her beloved great-great-grandmother. "I thank you, Bobe Malka, for everything that you have done for me. And I wish to thank all of you for making me feel welcome. I have been twice blessed. I know that my loving family is waiting for me at home, but I have been made to feel quite a part of this extraordinary tribe—from learning how to make gefilte fish, to battling out political disagreements, to picking out the perfect shoes, to studying Torah. I'm a changed person—a better person—for having known you." She felt a wave of tranquility come over her. It was like a warm embrace and she felt safe. More than that, she was ready to let go.

Molly finally realized that obsessing over her ancestors safety wouldn't change anything. Like the song said, '*Que será, será*; whatever will be, will be.' She lifted her glass and proposed a toast. "Whichever path you choose to take, wherever this life leads you, may God bless you and keep you safe."

Duvid shot up from his seat and raised his glass. "*L'chaim!*" he shouted.

The family responded in kind. Glasses were raised and a heartfelt, "To life!" was repeated by all. Blessings were said, the meal was served, and the room was a glow with love and laughter and good humor—even Avram and Bluma were in good spirits. *Was there a sparkle in Bluma's eye? Was Avram being charming?*

Molly's gaze went around the table, going from relative to relative, trying to ingrain their image in her memory. When her eyes came to Bobe Malka, she smiled an acknowledgment: *I'm okay.*

Later that evening, Malka walked with Molly towards her bedroom door. She leaned over to kiss her goodnight. "I am very proud of how you handled yourself, my dear."

"Thank you, Bobe. I just wish—I wish this wasn't so final."

"We will always be with you in spirit, and perhaps, this thought might help erase the finality of tonight's chapter. You now have in your possession all the names you had been seeking. When you return home, you will be better equipped to complete your research. Imagine how lovely your family tree will be now that you can fill in the empty branches. You will be able to follow each twig —each leaf and see what marvelous things they—we—were able to accomplish. And you will have the satisfaction of saying, 'I knew them when...'

"I have something to say about that."

"What is it, my dear?" the wise woman asked, happily noting the twinkle in the girl's eye.

"There is a saying in this country," Molly declared with a wide grin. "'There is no bad, without some good.'"

CHAPTER THIRTEEN

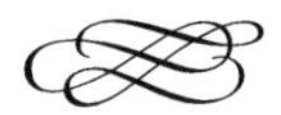

20th of April

It was a steadfast, but subdued group that gathered in the attic the following morning. Pale and just a tad nauseous, Molly was dressed again in her T-shirt and jeans. Leah and Duvid stood ghostly quiet off in a corner. Only Bobe Malka appeared stoic and ready for the proceedings. Reaching into her pocket, the matriarch withdrew the card, brushed it against her lips, and ceremoniously handed it to Molly.

"How do you know for certain that this will work?" Molly asked, not for the first time.

"Why should it not?" Malka replied. "You have accomplished a great many things. You have traveled far and have experienced an adventure. You have been presented with opportunities for growth. As we know, these are attributes of the card and now you must return to your own time. I have every faith that all will be well."

Leah and Duvid approached and said their goodbyes. The room was abuzz with tension. Each knew that, at any moment, tears would be unleashed and there would be no stopping the flood. It fell upon Malka to intervene.

"Let us recall this saying, my dears: 'Long parting ceremonies mean unnecessary tears.' I would not have us linger on the moment and make this departure even more bittersweet. Malyshka, you know what you must do. Simply read the incantation around the edges, as you did before, and...may God be with you."

"But—" Molly hesitated. This is what she wanted, wasn't it? She needed to go home and yet...

"Malyshka—please," her elder implored.

Molly held the card up to the candle and began reciting the mysterious words. The light began to flicker as she turned to say one last goodbye. She recognized the burning sensation at her fingertips the moment she fainted away.

"Moe-li? Moe-li! Vhat has happenedt here? Wake up malyshka!"

Molly gave herself a moment to acclimate to the brightness of the room. With a grimace, she warily opened her eyes. "Galina," she voiced wryly, "your shrieks could wake the dead."

Finding her legs a bit shaky, she hoisted herself up off the floor using the ancient steamer trunk for support. She looked about the room and recognized that she was indeed back in the attic-and it was 2015.

"I guess it worked," she said softly.

"Vhat vorkedt? Moe-li? Vhat happenedt to you? After I left

here, I vent to library in Great Choral Synagogue and didt research on Abramovitz family. Vhen you no return to hotel last night, I grew vorriedt. Vhen you no arrivedt at hotel this morning, I thought better I come to house, andt here I findt you—deadt to the vorldt!"

"I'm fine, Galina. It's a long story...wait—what did you say about last night?"

"I say you scaredt me when you no return to hotel last night. Vhere did you go? Vhat happenedt?" Galina screeched, waiving her ever-lit cigarette like Cruela deVille.

"Are you saying that the last time you saw me was yesterday afternoon?"

"Yes Moe-li. Vhat is matter? You no remember? You say to me, 'Galina, go home' and so, I didt. You hit your headt on something?"

"But I have been gone for weeks..."

"Moe-li, Moe-li! My little one. Come sit down andt drink vater," Galina insisted in her most maternal tone.

Molly obeyed. She was too stunned to do otherwise. *It's the Space Time continuum thing again!*

She leaned against the trunk and took another sip of water. Turning her head to rub a sore muscle, her eyes caught sight of the familiar book on Gematria. Lying next to it slightly eschew was a stack of papers prettily tied with a satin ribbon.

"Funny, I don't remember seeing this here before." She bent to pick it up, when she noticed yet another bundle.

Molly lifted the brown paper package and hurriedly untied the string. She gasped as the paper dropped away and revealed Rivka's white ball gown. A note was pinned on the bodice: *For Marina—When she finally decides to wed her Dr. Zhivago.*

With tear filled eyes, Molly looked again at the packet of

documents and untied the ribbon. The first sheet was a bill of sale for passage on the Sofia Hohenberg ocean liner. The port of departure was listed as Trieste. She recalled her father's stories, remembering tales of the family traipsing across Russia, but she had no idea that their journey had begun from an Austro-Hungarian port. Molly knew of the difficulties any Russian subject faced when trying to leave his community, let alone his country. Because of the many formalities, obtaining the necessary paperwork and passports was quite costly and time consuming. She surmised that emigration from Trieste might have been an easier process.

The document also noted that the ship's destination was the port of Buenos Aires, Argentina. The fact that it didn't list the passengers was a point of concern. Molly and her father weren't able to track all of the siblings in Argentina. She wondered exactly who made it on that ship. She looked onto the next document. It was Solomon's death certificate which not only detailed the date and cause of demise, but also indicated that the family were Kohanim. That was an extraordinary discovery.

"Of course! I remember now. I was overwhelmed with emotion at the time—"

The priestly benediction engraved on her great-great grandfather's tombstone—located on the outer edge of the park—was a tell-tale sign meant to honor a Kohan. There were stories which intimated that the family descended from this tribe, but it was a running joke among Jewish genealogists—everyone wanted to discovery their direct patrilineal descent from the biblical Aaron.

She now had a solid lead towards proving the supposition to her incredulous father. The next step would be DNA testing, as science discovered that a majority of present-day male descendants of the Kohanim shared certain markers. With Solomon's documentation in hand, her father would have his much-needed evidence that the testing was worthwhile.

Lastly, returning her attention to the packet, Molly found a letter from Bobe Malka. She felt her knees buckle and allowed herself to slide down to the floor. She glanced at Galina standing in the corner and gave her a teary grin.

"I'm alright," she said. "Just give me a moment." Taking a deep breath, she was now prepared.

My dear, we have a saying here, 'Every woman is a rebel, and she is usually in wild revolt against herself'. I hope that your rebellion has come to an end; that you allow yourself to be who you truly were meant to be. When you came to us, you had rejected your name. You spurned your purpose. Your perception of being Malka was not based on knowledge. You placed her on a royal pedestal, above reproach—beyond your grasp.

Malchut is not the Queen because she has all the strength or all the answers—quite the contrary. She is the last sephirah. She sits on the bottom of the Tree of Life. We are grounded in her base. Those who dwell on this physical plane dream of obtaining the Light of Keter believing that when they reach that shining crown, their journey is complete. Herein lies another misconception, my dear, for the true journey is within, not above or beyond.

This is your lesson; your strength comes from this Source. Your power stems from the roots of Malchut. Do not belittle what was learned here. Do not disparage the manner of the instruction. These blessings manifested for you; the lessons were meant to help you on your journey. I too have enclosed a gift. It is meant to help illuminate your path, my dear.

May Hashem bless you and keep you.

May His face shed light upon you and be gracious unto you.

May Hashem lift up His face unto you and give you peace.

Galina watched as Molly unrolled a length of linen to reveal a set of silver candlesticks, and although she was not aware of the contents of the letter, she realized that her young charge had been touched by something of great importance. Remembering suddenly that she too had found hidden treasure, Galina quickly went to Molly's side to share her discoveries.

"Moe-li, my dear, look here at vhat I foundt in library," she said, fitfully waving an official looking document in the young woman's face. "See here, all names of family and one orphaned, servant girl by the name of Gitel... all left Odessa. Look, here is date: April 4, 1901."

Molly sat there, surrounded by Rivka's gown, by Solomon's death certificate, the treasured candlesticks, Bobe Malka's words of wisdom and the defining proof that the family—all the family—escaped. They made it out. They survived. They *thrived*, and so would she, because she was well on her way to becoming Malka.

GLOSSARY OF TERMS

A

Anetevka: A fictional village in the movie, 'Fiddler on the Roof.'

Azoy: Yiddish; meaning Really; You don't say?

B

Baal Shem Tov: Rabbi Yisroel ben Eliezer was considered to be the founder of Hasidic Judaism.

Babe/Bobe: Yiddish/Slavic term for 'grandmother.' Vowel pronunciation varied from country to country. In the U.S., it is usually written as 'bubbe.'

Babe/Bobe/Bubbe Maises: Yiddish. Old wives or grandmothers' tales.

Baba Yaga: A controversial Eastern European 'witch' who is neither good, nor evil, known to help lost souls but requires a pure spirit and preparation before being addressed.

Babushka: A headscarf tied under the chin, typically worn by Polish and Russian women.

Bar Mitzvah: Hebrew meaning 'Son of the Commandments'. A rite of passage for a Jewish boy who, at the age of 13, is ready to observe religious precepts and eligible to take part in public worship. It is erroneous to say 'I was bar mitzvahed,' rather one should say, 'I am a Bar Mitzvah' or 'I became a Bar Mitzvah.' **Bat** Mitzvah refers to a Daughter of the Commandments.

Baruch Hashem: Hebrew idiom used commonly to say, 'Thank God.'

Beit Tefillah. Hebrew for House of Prayer.

Ben: Hebrew for 'son of', such as Isaac ben Abraham.

Benching/Birkat Hamazon: Hebrew; blessing (thanksgiving prayers) after the meal.

Boychik: Yiddish term for little man or young boy.

Bracha: Hebrew for blessing.

Bris: Hebrew; Also called Brit or Bris Milah (Covenant of Circumcision) is a ceremony during which a baby boy is brought into the Covenant of the Jewish people.

B'rit Bat: Hebrew; A ceremony of blessing and naming that celebrates the birth of a daughter and her entry into the covenant of the Jewish people.

Bund: The Jewish Labour Bund was a component of the social democratic movement until the Russian Revolution of 1917; later splitting due to internal differences between communist and socialist lines.

C

Cantonist: Jewish children who were conscripted to military service in czarist Russia for a term of 25 years. It was the intention to forcibly convert the children to Christianity. They were provided military training, as well as a rudimentary education. Discipline was maintained by threat of starvation and corporal punishment.

Challah: Hebrew; leavened egg bread, typically plaited, traditionally baked to celebrate the Sabbath.

Chazzan: Hebrew; Cantor-an official who sings liturgical music and leads prayer in a synagogue.

Crypto Jews: A.K.A. Converso, Marrano, New Christian: these titles, amongst others, are intermittently applied to the Jews of 15th-17th century Spain and Portugal who were forcibly converted to Catholicism under the threat of torture or death. Many converted publicly, but hid their Jewish way of life and therefore were known as crypto-Jews.

D

Dacha: Russian word for a country house or cottage, typically used as a second or vacation home.

Doctor Zhivago: Referring to the epic drama set in Russia between 1917-1922.

E

Eruv hatseroth: Hebrew; a ritual enclosure that some communities (ultra-Orthodox) construct in their neighborhoods as a way to permit residents to carry objects outside their own homes on Sabbath and Yom Kippur.

Eishet Chayil: Hebrew; A Woman of Valor; a prayer which is recited on the Sabbath.

Eretz Ysroel: Hebrew; The Land of Israel. In Ottoman/Turkish times, Eretz Ysroel was used to designate the area surrounding Jerusalem and including areas from the Litani River in the north to modern Eilat.

F

Fileteo/Fileteado: Castilian Spanish; Type of artistic, stylized, drawing typically used in Buenos Aires, Argentina.

Freylekh: Yiddish term for Eastern European Jewish music, a.k.a. Klezmer.

Frum: Yiddish; Meaning devout or pious.

G

Gregorian calendar: Internationally accepted civil calendar, also known as the 'Western calendar' or 'Christian calendar'

Gut Shabbes: Yiddish salutation meaning Good Sabbath.

H

Hamotzi: Hebrew; prayer recited before eating bread.

Hasidic/Hasidim: Hebrew; meaning piety or loving-kindness. A branch of Orthodox Judaism that promotes spirituality through the internalization of Jewish mysticism as the fundamental aspect of the faith.

Hashem: Hebrew; meaning The Name, referring to God. The Orthodox won't write the full name therefore, in English, it's common to see G-d.

Haskalah: Hebrew; A movement that brought the 'European Enlightenment' to the Jewish world in the 18th century. Jews were encouraged to study secular subjects, to learn European and Hebrew languages, and to enter fields such as agriculture, arts and science. Followers tried to assimilate into European society in dress, language, and manners.

Havdalah: Hebrew; a ceremony marking the end of the Sabbath, a separation between the sacred to the 'everyday'.

Hebrew calendar: A lunar calendar as opposed to the solar calendar. The numerical year on the Jewish calendar represents the number of years since Creation. It is not believed that the universe has existed for only 5700 +years, rather that our understanding of time is limited.

I

Idishke: Yiddish term for Jewish.

K

Kamishbroit: Yiddish; Almond cookies closely related to the biscotti. In the U.S., they are also known as mandelbroit or mandel bread.

Kardashians: 'Reality T.V.', tabloid family.

Kashrut/kosher: Hebrew; meaning suitable and/or pure, thus ensuring fitness for consumption. Dietary rules regulating which foods are permitted. Because Jewish law prohibits causing pain to animals, the slaughtering has to be effected in such a way that unconsciousness is instantaneous and death occurs almost instantaneously.

Kiddush/Kiddush cups: Hebrew; A ceremony of blessing over wine, performed by the head of a Jewish household at the meal ushering in the Sabbath or a holy day. Many families have a special glass or goblet, often an heirloom, but any cup can function as a Kiddush cup.

Kokoshnik: Russian; A traditional headdress. High front, shaped like a crescent with rounded edges, usually decorated with pearls, gems or coins.

Kohanim: Hebrew; Kohen or Cohen for priest- of direct patrilineal descent from the biblical Aaron.

L

Lada: Russian; Car manufactured in Russia circa 1970's.

Lashon Hara: Hebrew; Evil tongue/derogatory gossip.

Lvov: City currently in the western Ukraine. A.K.A. as Lviv, Lwów.

M

Malka: Hebrew; literally means queen.

Matushka: Russian term of endearment for mother.

Mezuzot/mezuzah: Hebrew; a parchment inscribed with religious texts and attached in a case to the doorpost of a Jewish house.

Misnagdim: Hebrew; Referring to opponents of Hasidism.

Mitzvah: Hebrew; literally meaning a commandment, used commonly as 'a good deed.'

Mohel: Hebrew; A person who performs Jewish circumcisions. They're required to have both religious and surgical training.

N

Naches: Yiddish; a term meaning joy, delight, pride.

O

Oy, gevalt: Yiddish; meaning woe is me, similar to the phrase 'Oy veys mir.'

P

Pale of Settlement: A territory within the borders of czarist Russia wherein the Jews were deprived of freedom of movement and confined to their places of residence.

Pesach: Hebrew; the Jewish holiday of Passover (recalling the Exodus from Egypt).

Peyot, peyes: Hebrew for sidelocks or sidecurls worn by some men and boys in the Orthodox community based on an interpretation of the Biblical injunction against shaving the 'corners' of one's head.

Po'alei Zion: Hebrew; a movement that consisted of a combination of Zionism and socialism.

Podstakannik: Russian for tea glass holder, most commonly made of metal.

Pogrom: Russian; an organized violence against Jews in Russia or Eastern Europe.

Polishe: Yiddish term for a Polish person or someone from the Galicia region.

S

Sandek: Hebrew; Person honored at the circumcision ceremony, traditionally either by holding the baby or by handing the baby to the mohel.

Sefer Yetziroh: Hebrew; Book of Formation or Creation, the earliest existing book on Jewish esotericism.

Shabbes/Shabbos: Yiddish for Sabbath.

Shabbes Queen: In Jewish literature, poetry and music, Shabbat is described as a bride or queen.

Shavua Tov: Hebrew; literally, good week. This greeting is used after

Havdalah.

Sheine meidelach: Yiddish for pretty girl.

Shema: The affirmation of Judaism and a declaration of faith in one God. Jewish law requires a greater measure of concentration on the first verse of the Shema; people commonly close their eyes or cover them with the palm of their hand while reciting it to eliminate every distraction and help them concentrate on the meaning of the words.

Shomer Shabbes: A person who observes the mitzvot (commandments) associated with Judaism's Sabbath which begins at dusk on Friday until sunset Saturday.

Shtetl: Yiddish for village or small town.

Sobremesa: Castilian Spanish; term for after dinner conversation.

T

Talmud: The body of Jewish civil and ceremonial law and legend comprising the Mishnah and the Gemara.

Tanakh: An acronym of the first Hebrew letter of each of the three traditional subdivisions: Torah (Teaching, also known as the Five Books of Moses), Nevi'im (Prophets) and Ketuvim (Writings)—hence TaNaKh.

Tarot: Cards used from the mid-15th century in various parts of Europe. The cards are traced by some historians to ancient Egypt or the Kabbalah.

Tatar: A member of the combined forces of central Asian peoples, including Mongols and Turks, under the leadership of Genghis Khan circa early 13th century.

Tevye: The main character in the film, 'Fiddler on the Roof.' Set in the Pale of Settlement in 1905 and based on Tevye and his Daughters by Sholem Aleichem.

Toilette: French; the process of washing oneself, dressing, and attending to one's appearance.

Torah: Hebrew; In its most limited sense, Torah refers to the Five Books of Moses: Genesis, Exodus, Leviticus, Numbers and Deuteronomy. Non-Jews refer to the Torah as the 'Old Testament.'

Tree of Life: *This explanation is, at best, a gross oversimplification. According to Kabbalah, the true essence of G-d is known as Ein Sof, which literally means 'without end.' The Ein Sof interacts with the universe through ten emanations, known as the Ten Sefirot, which make up the Tree of Life. The Sefirot correspond to qualities of G-d. They consist of Keter (crown), Chokhmah (wisdom), Binah (understanding), Chesed (mercy), Gevurah (strength), Tiferet (glory), Netzach (victory), Hod (majesty), Yesod (foundation) and Malkut (the queen).

Tzaddik: Hebrew; A righteous man.

Tzizit: Hebrew; knotted ritual fringes worn in antiquity by Israelites and today by observant Jews.

Y

Yenta: Yiddish name meaning noble; good-hearted; the name deteriorated to signify a well-intentioned woman who is in everyone's business.

Yeshiva/yeshivot: Hebrew; an institution that focuses on the study of traditional religious texts, primarily the Talmud and Torah study.

Yiddish: At one time, Yiddish was the international language of Ashkenazi (the Jews of Central and Eastern Europe). A hybrid of Hebrew and medieval German and many other modern languages.

Z

Zeide: Yiddish term meaning grandfather.

Zionist: A movement that supports the re-establishment of a Jewish homeland in the territory defined as the historic Land of Israel.

BOOK CLUB QUESTIONS

As much as I would love to meet with all of you, I unfortunately am lacking a mythical tarot card to transport to your next book club gathering. Instead, I will provide you with a few questions to ponder at your convenience. Maybe you could send a message or post your response on my Facebook page. I'd love to hear your thoughts!

Molly knew she was named for her great-great-grandmother, Malka. Were you named in honor of a beloved ancestor? Is it important to know? Does it affect how you act or carry yourself...how you live your life?

What was your initial reaction to the fantasy element surrounding the tarot card? How do you feel about Jewish mysticism in general?

Bobe Malka urges Molly not to put her ancestors on pedestals. In fact, she said, "We are human beings with faults and weakness like everyone else." Can you relate to Molly's feelings of being less than capable of filling her ancestor's shoes? If so, which qualities do you most admire and aspire to emulate in your relatives?

Did you grow up hearing "babe maises"-old wives tales? What are some of the most outrageous? Are there any that ring true today? Are we too quick to disregard "ancient wisdoms?"

Are you an "Olympic gold medalist" creator of lists like Molly? Do you think she was finally able to "let it go" and incorporate a bit of spontaneity into her must-be-in-control-at-all-times lifestyle?

Following the "queen theme," Disney's Queen Elsa reminds me a little bit of Molly. Does liberation from restriction and judgment resonate with you?

Duvid asked, "Why are adults so eager to dismiss things that they cannot explain?" Can you—do you—make allowances for things that are inexplicable?

On several occasions, Molly found herself railing against the restrictions placed on her female ancestors. She asks an interesting question. Is it fair to put a generation of Victorian-era women under a 21st century microscope in order to judge their actions and accomplishments? Do you find yourself doing the same thing when studying biblical women such as Sara, Rebecca, Leah, Rachel, etc.? Do we tend to think of our matriarchs in terms of modern-day women and feel that they were treated unfairly—unjustly?

AUTHOR'S NOTES

I hope you enjoyed Molly's journey in *Becoming Malka*. It is a story that rings true—except for the time travel—as I am a Jewish, Russian, Argentine, American immigrant myself! I wrote a Creative Nonfiction that speaks to the impetus of my family's exodus to America; namely a Peronista government, a stagnant economy and an anti-Semitic culture. The family transform into jet-setters relentlessly traveling back and forth across the continents thanks to a mother that never stops crying about 'The Argentina Family' and a father who works for Pan American Airlines.

With Love, The Argentina Family-Memories of Tango and Kugel; Mate with Knishes, is a coming-of-age memoir. Follow the sometimes comical, sometimes poignant trials and tribulations of a girl coming to terms with her Jewish heritage, her Argentine traditions and her fierce American patriotism. My books are available on Amazon in both electronic and paperback formats.

Look for me on: Goodreads, Instagram, Bookbub, Pinterest and on my blog: www.mirtainestruppauthor.com

I am grateful to my family and friends, fellow Indie authors and beta readers from across the globe. Thank you for sharing my journey.

With love,

~Mirta

ALSO BY MIRTA INES TRUPP

With Love, The Argentina Family~

Destiny by Design~ Leah's Journey

The Meyersons of Meryton

Celestial Persuasion

Made in the USA
Middletown, DE
16 May 2023